THE EASTERN BREW

THE EASTERN BREW

An Assortment of stories from East

Translated And Edited

SYED SARWAR HUSSAIN

PARTRIDGE
A Penguin Random House Company

ISBN:	Hardcover	978-1-4828-1255-8
	Softcover	978-1-4828-1256-5
	Ebook	978-1-4828-1254-1

To order additional copies of this book, contact
Partridge India
000 800 10062 62
www.partridgepublishing.com/india
orders.india@partridgepublishing.com

CONTENTS

dedicated to the memory of my parents-in-law

A pervading feeling of gratitude towards my parents steers through the course of this anthology—a force that had inspired me with courage and conviction throughout my corporeal as well as intellectual journey during the months this book took to write.

ACKNOWLEDGEMENTS

This book has evolved over a considerable period of time. And during its slow and often interrupted evolution I have accumulated many debts, only a few of which I have space to acknowledge here.

I would like to express my greatest gratitude to the writers, their legal heirs, and Mr. Imtiaz Karimi, Secretary, Bihar Urdu Academy (India), for the stories that they so graciously allowed me to translate and publish in this anthology. A special thank of mine goes to Mr. Syed Masood Hasan, from the Khuda Bakhsh Oriental Library, one of the premier national libraries of India, to help me in collecting stories for translation, and for his continuous support.

Above all I want to thank my wife, and the rest of my family, who supported and encouraged me in spite of all the time it took me away from them. It was a long and difficult journey for them.

I would like to thank Ms. Jireh InGod my Publishing Consultant, Ms. Ann Minoza, Publishing Services Associate with Partridge Publishing for helping me in talking things over, and the efficient and supportive team at Partridge Publishing, India, for their remarks and assistance in the editing, proofreading and design, enabling me to publish this book.

I would like to express my gratitude to the many people who saw me through this book; to all those who provided support, read, wrote, offered comments, over the course of years.

1. PHOTOGRAPHER

Qurratul Ain Haider

The extremely beguiling guest house is visible from a distance, perched on a verdant hilltop surrounded by a girdle of fresh spring flowers. A bubbling mountain lake runs down the hillock and a narrow track winds its way up along this lake reaching all the way to the gate of the guesthouse. A photographer with a walrus moustache sits indolently in a metal chair near the gate, his equipment lying on the ground beside him. This relatively unknown mountain town is off the usual tourist route and, therefore, is rarely frequented by regular travellers. If perchance some honeymooning couple or traveller wanders towards the guesthouse, the waiting photographer gets up and starts walking on the garden path, holding his camera with hope and patience. There is an unspoken understanding between him and the gardener that the latter will beckon him when going to present a morning bouquet of flowers to the guests, preferably the young ladies. And when the young damsels walk down to the garden after their breakfast, they find the gardener and the photographer waiting vigilantly for them.

The photographer has been here a long time. He refuses to go anywhere else and establish his own permanent studio. This is his birthplace. The hills and lakes belong to him. Why should he leave them? He has spent his life here quietly, watching the myriad colours of a changing world. The earliest visitors to the guesthouse, in his memory, were the '*sahibs*', the British planters, wearing white sun hats, the wives of arrogant officers in the colonial service, and their children. They would spend their nights upstairs drinking heavily like horses, while the gramophone blared maddeningly. The wooden floor of the drawing room downstairs was reserved for dancing. During the Second World War, the Americans started coming.

And then the country won independence.

The visitors to the guesthouse now are occasional tourists, government officers, newlywed couples, or painters and artists in search of solitude—people who want to capture the sight of colourful rainbows arching over the lake on rainy evenings. They are seekers of everlasting love and peace—two passions that are out of stock in our temporal life. Our mortal existence, as it is, is closely followed by death at its heels. It goes with us wherever we go. It is our constant fellow traveller.

Tourists keep coming and going and the vigilant eye of the photographer's camera captures everything around silently, secretly.

One evening a young man and a young woman landed at the guesthouse. They did not appear to have come for their honeymoon. They looked quite happy but serious as they carried their luggage to their suite on the first floor. The entire floor was empty. There was a dining hall near the staircase, and three bedrooms in a row joined by a common sitting room.

"I'll take this one", the young man said, entering the first room, whose windows looked out toward the lake. The young woman dumped her umbrella and overcoat on the bed in the room.

"Take your things away!" the young man snapped.

"Okay, fine!" The young woman picked her things and went through the sitting room to another room which had a tiled passageway at the back. From the large windows of the room, labourers could be seen climbing a ladder, busy fixing the back wall.

A porter brought her luggage to the room, closed the curtains, and left. She changed her clothes and came back to the sitting room. The young man was sitting in an armchair near the fireplace writing something. He lifted his eyes and looked at her. Outside, darkness had suddenly started to spread over the lake. She went near the windows and gazed at a rainbow arching over the garden. When it grew darker she gave up looking at the rainbow and moved toward the young man, settling into the chair beside him. They started talking. Down near the gate, the photographer was still waiting for them. His camera had eyes but no ears.

By that time a European tourist had also entered the guesthouse. He was now sitting quietly in another corner of the sitting room, writing letters. Some picture postcards lay in front of him on the table.

"Look there! That tourist must be writing to his wife back home telling her that at the moment he's in the mystifying East, at a mysterious *Dak Bungalow*. And that a mysterious Indian girl clad in a red sari is sitting in front of him. It's an incredibly romantic atmosphere . . ." the young woman whispered, and her companion gave a short, amused laugh.

The two of them went to the dining room for dinner. They returned to the sitting room after some time and sat together. The young man was now reading something to her. The night had worn on. Suddenly, the young woman sneezed loudly.

She felt uneasy and, drawing a tremulous breath through her nose, pronounced "We should go to sleep now!"

The young man reminded her, "Don't forget to take your medicine!"

"O yes, thanks! Good night!" she replied and went to her room. The passageway at the back was bathed in darkness. The room was pretty quiet, cozy, and comfortable. Life too had been quite peaceful and easy for her. She changed into her nightdress, and was taking her medicine out of the dressing table drawer when there was a knock at the door. She slipped into her black kimono and opened the door. Her young companion was standing there nervously.

He quickly uttered, "Sorry, but I too have started getting a nasty cough!"

"Really?" the young woman looked surprised, and gave him the cough syrup and a spoon. The young man dropped the spoon on the floor, picked it up, and walked out to his room. The young girl switched the lights off and went to sleep.

The next morning, she got ready and walked to the dining hall for her breakfast. The fragrant smell of fresh flowers was floating in the air in the hall. Huge, brightly polished, brass vases stood in a neat row on the glittering hardwood floor. Bunches of fresh, brightly coloured flowers were lying near the vases. The lake outside was sparkling in the light of the morning sun and yellow and white butterflies were fluttering across the lush green garden. After some time the young man appeared coming up the stairs to the hall. He was laughing and held a bouquet of flowers in his hands.

He entered the hall and held the bouquet out to the young woman. Smiling up at her, he said, "The gardener has sent this for you. He's standing downstairs."

She picked out a tiny flower out of the bunch, stuck it carelessly in her topknot, and started flipping through the morning newspaper.

The young man continued his speech, "A photographer is also hanging around downstairs. He asked me very seriously whether you weren't a certain film star!"

The young man sat down on a chair near the tea table and started making tea. The young woman couldn't stop laughing. In truth, she was a very famous dancer and the young man was an even more celebrated musician. But nobody recognized them there. They were enjoying their temporary anonymity and quiet solitude at the guesthouse enormously.

The European tourist, taking his breakfast in another corner of the dining hall, looked at them and smiled. He had also joined in their quiet happiness.

After breakfast the young couple went down to the garden and stood together under the *gulmohar* tree on one side of the garden, watching the winding lake.

All of a sudden, the photographer appeared as if from nowhere, bowed to them removing his hat in a very dramatic way, and inquired, "Photographer, lady?"

The young woman looked at her watch and said, "I'm sorry! We have to leave right now or it will be too late."

"Kind lady," the photographer placed one foot on the coping of the low garden wall, and stretching his hands out towards the world outside, continued, "A furious fight is raging on the battleground of life. I know you've broken out of the battleground to steal some moments of happiness in the peaceful atmosphere here. Listen, the rainbow over the lake is going to vanish in seconds. But, don't worry; I won't take much of your time. Please, come closer for a second!"

"The man appears to be a very eloquent speaker!" she said softly to her companion.

The gardener, as if waiting for his chance, emerged from behind another *gulmohar* tree nearby and, darting forward, presented a bouquet to the young woman. She broke into peels of laughter and moved near the life-size statue of *Parvati*—the Hindu god Shiva's consort, at the end of the garden for a picture with her friend. She squinted her eyes against the strong glare of the sun and smiled faintly.

'*Click, click*!' The photographer quickly took their picture.

"You'll get your pictures in the evening. Thank you lady . . . thank you sir!" The photographer bowed again and touched his hat.

The two young people walked down towards their car.

They returned late in the evening after their outing, flopped down into the garden chairs placed on the grass outside, and stayed there awhile in the mellow evening light. When the evening mist started rolling over the grass, they moved to the quiet, spacious drawing room on the ground floor and fell into a long, hushed conversation in the gentle light of the orange, hanging lamp shades. After dinner, they went up to their rooms. Both of them were leaving early the next morning and were so engrossed in their conversation that they forgot to retrieve their pictures from the photographer.

The young woman was still in her room in the morning when the room boy entered and handed an envelope to her.

"This is for you, madam. The photographer gave it to me last night" the room boy said.

"Fine! Leave it in the drawer over there!" She gestured to him carelessly and started arranging her hair.

When she was packing up she didn't remember to take the envelope out of the drawer and, casting a fleeting glance around the room, walked out to the car. The young man was waiting for her there. As they sped off, the photographer got up and saluted them. They waved back to him, and the car ran down the slope of the hill and vanished.

The photographer with the walrus moustache has now grown old. But he continues sitting in his metal chair near the gate, taking pictures of the tourists at the guest house. With the expansion of new air services, these days, their numbers have increased considerably.

But as it was a lean season, that day when the tourist coach entered the guesthouse gate it had only one passenger—a woman well past her prime. When the bus stopped at the entrance portico, the woman got off, holding a suitcase, looking quizzically at the photographer. The poor man rose quickly from his chair, but slumped down into it dejectedly when he found that the centre of his attention was not a young woman but a lady well into middle age.

The lady entered the guesthouse office, registered her arrival, and went up to the room allotted to her. The guesthouse was quite deserted. A tourist group had just left the place for an onward destination and the cleaners had set the entire place back in order. The brass vases standing on the polished wooden floor of the hall, waiting for fresh flowers, were still shining brightly. The beautiful silver knives and forks on the bright white table under the French window in the dining hall had not yet lost their original sparkle. The lady passed by the middle room and went to her own at the end of the passage. She dropped off her baggage there and went straight out to have a good look at the lake. She returned to the empty sitting room after quite some time, stayed there for almost an hour, and then went back to her own room.

When the lengthening shadows from the passage peeped into her room, she got up and walked over to the window and looked out to find that, after having toiled the whole day, the laborers had left the ladder leaning against the wall. The passage too was completely abandoned. She went back to her bed and was going to stretch out when she heard a sudden knock at the door. When she opened it she found no one there. The sitting room was strangely still and silent. She closed the door and while returning to her bed felt that the room had suddenly become extremely cold.

The next morning she packed her suitcase and went over to the dressing table to do her hair. Pulling the drawer open accidentally, she discovered an envelope with her name written on it under a transparent yellow spread sheet. Amazed, the lady took it out instantly. A cockroach fell onto her palm from underneath the envelope. She jerked her hand violently out of sudden fear, and a picture fell out of the envelope. It showed a young man and a young woman smiling gently, standing near the statue of *Parvati*. The paper had yellowed but the photo was intact. The lady kept looking at the picture, rapt in deep thought, and then put it into her purse.

Meanwhile, the room boy announced from outside that her airport coach was ready to leave. She came down with her suitcase and found the photographer walking on the garden path, looking for new tourists.

The lady went near him and spoke quite frankly, "Look, isn't it strange? The dressing table upstairs must have been cleaned many times during the past fifteen years, but this photograph has been left there in the drawer untouched."

Her voice suddenly thickened with anger, "It's quite disgusting how maintenance and upkeep has gone down through the years. There're cockroaches all over the place in the rooms."

The photographer looked at her flabbergasted, and tried to recognize her. Unable to recognize the woman through her wrinkled face, he turned his face the other way. The woman continued pouring out her verbal disgust over the state of affairs there. Her voice had changed, her face appeared rough and hard, and her manners betrayed fretfulness and displeasure.

She continued her tirade in her shrill, hoarse voice, "I've retired from the stage. Who would be interested in taking my photo now? No one, for sure! I just stayed here last night on my way home. The new air service to my town has started now and this place falls on the route. I had no other option."

"And . . . and . . . the young man with you . . . ? The photographer asked her softly.

The coach horn honked.

"Don't you remember, you told us yourself that a furious fight is raging on the battleground of life? He's lost in that furious battle. I couldn't find him anywhere."

The coach honked again.

"It has been ages since I lost him . . . Goodbye, then!" The lady cut the conversation short and hurried towards the coach.

Stupefied, the photographer with the walrus moustache returned mechanically to his seat near the gate of the guest house.

Life has devoured the human beings. Only the cockroaches are going to survive.

2. THE SEER AND THE BUTCHER

Intezar Husain

Long, long ago, there was a seer called *Kaushika*[1]. Though a good old seer, he was in actual fact a very irascible man. And so fierce was his wrath that those who met his furious, flaming gaze were burnt to coals. The seer would then regret why he burnt the poor fellow away. Once when he was sitting under a *holy* fig tree, lost in profound meditation, an ill-fated swan, exhausted after a long non-stop flight, descended on the lush green tree, shedding its droppings as it alighted on a branch.

The seer was engrossed in his contemplation right under the same branch. The droppings landed directly on his holy head, interrupting his meditation. The wise man fumed with rage and looked up. *So, it was the swan's doing*! The seer thought, and cast such a fierce look at it that the poor bird burnt into a lump of coal, and dropped to the ground in front of him.

After punishing the swan thus for its sin, his anger faded, replacing it with an overpowering feeling of remorse. *O, miserable bird! How could have it stopped its crap? It hadn't, after all, committed any sin heinous enough to claim its life. A fool that I was, I realized little what I was going to do. Ah, I've taken the poor swan's life*!

Seer *Kaushika* grieved greatly over burning the luckless bird. Struck with deep repentance, he made a firm intention to control his anger. But, as was his wont, he remembered nothing whenever anger inflamed him, and regretted later at his blind rage.

One day he left his ashram to collect *dakshina*[2]. On his round of a nearby village, he reached a house and tapped on the door. The mistress of the house was washing the dishes. She looked out from her kitchen window, and saw an old man with white matted hair standing in the doorway, carrying a spouted vessel in his hand.

Realizing a yogi had come for *dakshina*, she called out to him, "*Maharaj*[3], have patience please! I'm going to serve you as soon as I finish my dishwashing."

The seer squatted down in front of the door and started waiting. Inside, the cleaning and the washing of the dishes seemed never to end. The woman finally finished her kitchen chores, when the master of the house returned from work. She left all other jobs and threw herself into the service of her husband, washing his feet in a trough half-filled with water, bringing him food and drink, and waving a hand fan to cool him as it was a very hot day, while the indifferent man enjoyed his food peacefully.

After eating his bellyful, without uttering a word, he went to sleep. The work stress off her mind now, the woman suddenly recalled that the seer was waiting for her. She took the *dakshina* and rushed to the doorway. Finding him still sitting there, she pleaded. "Please forgive me, *maharaj*! I'm so sorry; you had to wait rather long! I was so busy doing my household chores that I forgot there was a sage gracing my house, squatting at the door."

Seer *Kaushika* was already fretting with anger over the inordinate delay. The woman's excuses further enraged him, and he retorted angrily, "So you remembered your wifely duties, eh! But lady, you forgot your religious duty to serve a visiting Brahmin? Didn't it cross your mind for once that I've been hunkering down at your door? Mind you, I'm not a beggar. I am a Brahmin!"

The woman stared at him open-mouthed, and suddenly recognized that it was seer *Kaushika*, the notoriously hot-tempered sage, seething with wrath. She instantly touched his feet, and pleaded with folded hands, "Revered sage! Please forgive me! I've made a great mistake!"

But the seer's anger refused to cool down. It had already reached the boiling point.

When she noticed that his wrath continued unabated, crossing all limits, she too retaliated in the same manner, "Don't cross your limits, O sage! You needn't vent your fury on me! I'm not a swan. Your wrath can't burn me out. I'm the wife of a Brahmin, and it's my duty to serve my husband. There is no duty greater than that. Look at the brambles and nettles you're carrying on your head! No big wonder if a swan pooped on it!"

The seer never expected in his dreams that one could dare speak to him like that. He wondered who that Brahmin woman was! He was extremely puzzled how she came to learn about the swan incident. Unable to hide his astonishment, he spoke out, "Hey woman, you've got very tetchy! How did you know about the swan's burning?"

She replied, "O sage, nothing remains hidden for long! You've burnt so many innocent birds with your flaming fury! How long could this lie unknown? Knowledge isn't only confined to the Vedas and *Puranas*[4]! It's incomplete without the awareness of the self, of your own human self. Of what use is the sage who commits all Vedas to memory, but fails to display perseverance?"

The seer stood up, his hands clasped together, "You win, hey *Brahmini*! And I lose! Now, I'm going to take lessons from you."

"I'm not a teacher or a preacher, sage *Kaushika*. I don't have much free time beyond my household duties. Besides, I know nothing about teaching. Why don't you go to *Mithila*[5], and sit at the foot of Dharam Viyadah, if you wish to attain knowledge? He will tell you the difference between *Dharma*[6] and *Adharma*."

The sage, with the name Dharam Viyadah in his mind, left the place as soon as he could, and marched towards *Mithila*.

Upon reaching *Mithila*, he enquired about the ashram of Dharam Viyadah. But he couldn't find it, as there was no such ashram there.

Everyone there expressed their ignorance, until he met an old inhabitant, who asked him, "Are you looking for Dharam Viyadah, the man himself?"

"O yes, exactly!"

"But Dharam Viyadah is a butcher! Why should he have an ashram? He has a butcher's shop! It's over there, at the end of the next lane!"

So Dharam Viyadah was a butcher! The news confounded and bewildered the seer. He told the man that he didn't believe him.

The elderly fellow responded, "I've given you his address. It's now up to you to do what you like."

The baffled seer hesitated for a while, and then decided to find out the truth. He walked to the bend of the next street and saw a meat shop. A brawny butcher was sitting on a low small stool with a cleaver in his hand. He was chopping lumps of meat into small pieces. The seer was filled with repulsion at the unpleasant sight, and felt that the butcher was certainly not the same Dharam Viyadah, the Brahmin woman had told him about. He was engrossed in his thoughts when the butcher's eyes fell on him. The fellow came out of his shop and touched the seer's feet, seeking his blessings.

"O holy sage! I know, the Brahmin lady has sent you here. I've been waiting for you, *maharaj*! Let's go to my house."

When they reached the butcher's house, the seer, utterly perplexed, felt as if he had reached the dream world of peace and tranquillity. The moment he entered his house, the butcher appeared no longer as a slaughterer of animals. He looked like an apostle of love, peace, and piety. And when he spoke, immortal words of wisdom and learning, with which even the seer was hitherto unfamiliar, flowed out of his mouth, like fresh spring showers. A thought pricked seer *Kaushika's* mind, uneasily like a thorn. *Why was such a profoundly wise man working as a butcher*?

His thoughts finally rolled off his tongue, "*Maharaj*, I am still amazed at what I am seeing now!"

"What's that?" asked the butcher

"How could a person with your wisdom, and your deep and extensive knowledge of the Vedas and *Shastras*[7], slaughter animals? A savant making a living from chopping animal flesh and selling it?" the seer expressed with surprise.

Dharam Viyadah laughed and replied, "O reverend sage, the whole universe, our entire life, is a strange spectacle revolving round the existential reality. All herbs and spices, crops and plants, and birds and animals, are ultimately eaten up whether or not you yourself pluck out their lives. Listen, O saint! There was a king in the ancient time. His name was *Raja Unt Deva*. He was a very kind and virtuous king. Every day thousands of animals were slaughtered for his kitchen. Two thousand of them were cows alone. But all that meat was never cooked in his kitchen. A very large portion of it was distributed among the poor and the needy."

"Even cows?" the seer's eyes flew open in surprise, "Oh, that's outrageous!"

"Hey sage, every living form is food for the other. The secret of life is shrouded in this reality."

Seer *Kaushika* contemplated seriously for some time, and then said thoughtfully, "O wise man, aren't you a Brahman?"

"I was once, but not now! I'm, nevertheless, going to become a Brahman again."

"I couldn't quite get you."

"Good saint, I was a Brahmin in my previous life, well-versed in the *Vedas* and *Shastras.* But I became friends with a king. He took me whenever he went hunting for games. The king had hunted and killed a lot of deer. Aping him, one day I too fired an arrow at a deer. But when I heard a shrill shriek, I realized to my horror that it had struck a human, and that too a sage. He threw a curse at me denouncing me to be reborn as a butcher. Afflicted by the sage's curse, I asked him how it was possible for me to enter into a butcher's skin leaving my Brahmin one. He said that the soul is a moving resident and can reside into any body whatsoever. And when I asked him how I could get back into my own Brahmin skin, he told me it would be only possible when I'd teach words of wisdom and learning to a sage. So, that was how my soul left my body and entered into a butcher's. But now that I have passed on my knowledge and wisdom to a sage, I will go back to my Brahmin skin. You are, therefore, going to become a butcher now, and I will turn into a Brahmin."

"How can I come back into my own skin?" Seer *Kaushika* asked clearly worried.

"You will get your skin back when you will impart knowledge to a self-proclaimed false saint like you, sitting at your feet. You will then regain your Brahmin skin, and he will assume the form of a butcher."

As Dharam Viyadah uttered this, he was transformed into a Brahmin, and seer *Kaushika* was changed into a butcher.

References

1. A Hindu *rishi* (saint) also known by the name of *Vishvamitra*, literally meaning 'friend of the universe'.
2. Holy oblation offered to a Brahman.
3. A respectful Hindi term for saints and sages.
4. Hindu religious scriptures
5. A city in ancient India, capital of the *Videha* Kingdom.
6. Dharma means *Law* or *Natural Law* and is a concept of central importance in Indian philosophy and culture.
7. *Śāstra* is Sanskrit for rules in a general sense. In essence, the *sastra or shaastra* is the knowledge which is based on principles that are held to be timeless.

3. BOREDOM

Akhtar Urainvi

A scruffy looking young man emerged into the porch, and ascending the stairs, stopped at the veranda in front of the drawing room.

"Is Dr. Joseph around—?"

Miss Nancy Santanam, sitting near the radio set in the drawing room, got up on hearing a strange voice, and saw a man standing awkwardly at the doorway. She watched him quietly. The man was very simply dressed—a grubby white shirt, white loose jeans badly creased, and a pair of old slippers on his feet. His face was rough and unshaven, and his hair unkempt. Miss Nancy and the stranger stood face to face staring at each other.

The newcomer, looked straight in Nancy's dark, deep-set, slanting eyes, and repeated his question, "Can I see Dr. Joseph Santanam?"

A sudden stillness seemed to take possession of Dr. Santanam's pleasant bungalow. The soothing song, emanating from the radio kept in a tidy corner of the room, sounded like the soft inland murmur of waters, rolling from their mountain-springs. Nancy, tall and graceful, stood still like a cypress tree, with her sari coiling around her body, and her long, thick hair hanging loose about her shoulders. In the compound, tamarisk and eucalyptus trees rose majestically, bathed in rain. It had just stopped raining. Nothing moved in the still air. The birds were still lying hidden in their nests. Nature had lapsed into a sullen silence. And Nancy too was quiet.

"I want to see Dr. Santanam! Is he at home?" the stranger spoke a little loudly.

Nancy didn't speak, but just shook her head from side to side.

"No one at home? Not even Mrs. Santanam?"

"No!"

The man's eyes betrayed a playful intrepidity, and there was a peculiar frankness in his tone. It looked as if he had decided to leave only after meeting someone in the house. Nancy wanted to tell him sternly that there was no one there and he could not meet anybody. She liked to be left alone, engrossed in the songs, passing the sad evening uneventfully. The stranger's interference was badly irritating her. But she was a civilized girl. So she replied with just a 'no' and thought that she had got herself out of the trouble.

"Can I get a piece of paper, please? It will be quite indecent to go back without meeting him. When do you expect him back?" the man persisted, and walked downright into the drawing room.

He was now standing beside Nancy, surveying her form, with total concentration.

"He'll be back not later than nine or ten, in the evening, or even later . . . !" she replied in great anxiety.

"Oh, then I must leave a note. I regret not meeting him today. He is my benefactor. May I have a pen and paper?" The man said, confidently settling his long frame down on the sofa, searching his pocket for a pen.

Nancy walked out into an adjacent room, creating a bend of displeasure in her lissome, graceful figure. The stranger was gazing out of the elegant drawing room, beyond the compound, away from the bordering lush greenery, across the river, at the emerald mountains. Dark, gray clouds were spreading their shadows on the damp earth. A refreshing cool wind was blowing on the high plains of *Chhotanagpur*[1], and gathering clouds like black, unchained, inebriated elephants swayed over the area; as the long black flowing locks, of a damsel drenched in youthful innocence, had fallen loose on her chest tossing sideway. And suddenly, it started drizzling.

The radio had stopped playing songs. It was broadcasting a feature now. Nancy returned to the drawing room quite annoyed. Handing out the letter pad and pen to the stranger, she resumed her place near the radio, and indifferent to the man's presence, lent her exclusive concentration to the broadcast. She clearly appeared distressed.

The stranger started writing his letter, but stopped midway, and turning to Nancy, spoke out, "Perhaps, you didn't recognize me. Nine years have passed, full nine years. You were then just about eleven years old. You're Nancy, perhaps! O yes, you are certainly Nancy! I can't be wrong in recalling those big, magnetic eyes. And where is Fancy? Your shy sister, Fancy! She was just ten years old doll. And Julian? He must have grown to be a handsome young man! Tell me, how's Defrin? . . ."

The deepening lines of concern etched into Nancy's brow were fainting now. She began watching the stranger with half-open eyes. Perhaps he was now no more a complete stranger to her.

"But I never imagined Nancy would turn out to be such an attractive and graceful woman. Oho, look how much you resemble your mother! Are you sure, you're really Nancy?"

The letter pad sat on the man's lap, and the pen was drowsing. His questions have again stopped his all other activities. A soft smile played on Nancy's smooth and lovely face. And the dimples in her cheeks appeared more prominent.

"Indeed you're Nancy! Aren't you? I know these dimples well."

Smile changed into laughter.

"Yes, I'm Nancy."

"You resemble your mother so much. These dimples . . ."

Cutting him short, Nancy answered, "Oh no! I don't take after my mother much. Actually, I have my father's height."

"O yes, you're tall like him. So fairly and fittingly tall! Besides, you're so gracefully when you walk, just like your father. Your complexion is even fairer than

Mrs. Santanam's. Perhaps you look more like your aunt. But yes, your height . . ."

"Well, I thank my God for that. I never liked to be short," replied Nancy, turning off the radio.

She was in good spirits now, and her cheerful face had become cheerier. She arranged the *pallu*[2] of her sari, and wrapping it tight over her chest continued the talk, "You haven't yet introduced yourself!"

"I'm Farhat, your family's old acquaintance. Dr. Santanam has been my guru, my guide. I can never forget his favours. More than just a physician, he has always been my consoler, my confidant. And in fact, Mrs. Santanam's care and support has been vital for my survival. How homely was life at the Health Centre! I really felt like a member of Dr. Santanam's family. Don't you remember Farhat? Have you forgotten the plays that we used to stage every month? Fancy, and Julian, and you, always mimicked my acting!"

"Aha! So you're that Farhat! There were two people with that name. I still recall those days. Picnic and whist playing, and Christmas celebrations! And of course the chirping nurses. I know, you were so interested in acting! You always entertained us with your amusing talks and jests. The other Farhat was fond of photography. And then there were Gupta, Kamla, David, Anwar, Miss D'Silva, and Miss Sihna, all very nice people. I wish those old days return!" Nancy recounted with a sense of nostalgia and regret.

"I'll come again, tomorrow. I must meet Dr. Santanam. You didn't, by the way, tell me anything about Fancy, Julian and Defrin. Where are they?"

"Julian's in his third year at the Madras Medical College. He left only day before yesterday, after spending his vacation here. Why don't you take some drink?"

Nancy went to bring him some drink, and Farhat resumed writing his letter.

"I hope you like orange squash! Here it is!" She held the glass out to him, entering the room.

"O, thanks a lot! Sorry for the trouble!"

"That's OK, Mr. Farhat. But what are you writing?" Nancy asked him with great interest.

"Miss Nancy, I'm a free lance journalist. Travelling and writing are my vocations."

"That's great! But are you interested in films? I love them. Fancy and I wished to see a film today, but mummy and daddy went to their Health Clinic. I'd to stay home to look after Defrin. One has to be here for him all day. He's such a naughty boy! He refused to listen to me and went out cycling in rain only moments ago, leaving me to boredom and loneliness. There's no social life here. This mountain township is so dull and desolate! I hate staying here. Sad evenings, dull mornings, forlorn days, and lifeless, unpleasant nights, oh my God!" There was a surge of annoyance in Nancy's voice.

"Too bad, really! Well now, tell me about those nine years that I was away from all of you. I'm dying to hear how you got along all those years." Farhat requested, taking a sip of the orange juice.

"You know, after leaving the management of the Health Centre, daddy stayed here, for some years. We all, then went to *Puna*[3], and he took charge of a Health Clinic there. We were sent to Bombay for our education. During those years Mr. Lingam looked after this bungalow. Mummy paid occasional visits to this town. Daddy came back here almost a year ago. I don't know why he feels so attached to this place. He doesn't want to leave it for good. He's now establishing his new Health Centre a few miles from here. But I'm mad about Bombay, and of course, its great evenings. I did my B.A. from Bombay University this year, and came back from there only two months ago. Fancy came here before me. She's now preparing for her Senior Cambridge, and I'm rotting at home. O, it's disgusting! I'm asking daddy to get me into Lady Irwin College at Delhi. I'd like to take a course in Cultural Studies or Domestic Science. I can't continue living morbidly anymore . . ." She suddenly checked herself, and fell silent as if she had unconsciously revealed an intimate secret.

She threw her head back in a very impressive manner. Her long curly hair, forming into a new pattern, tossed out of her face. Her well-developed body looked like plump South Indian cardamoms. The fragrance of southern breeze escaped out of her locks. Lustrous, slanting *Ajantan*[4] eyes, intoxicated with longings and restlessness hidden behind their feminine modesty, appeared like two brimming goblets of double distilled liquor.

"Why don't you entertain yourself with films . . . and mountain trekking? This is a very beautiful and interesting place." Farhat suggested.

He was staring at her with courage and interest. Nancy seemed to like his strong searching gaze. She felt as if she had been waiting for those inquisitive and intense eyes since early evening, or might be for months.

Farhat talked on non stop, admiring mountains, meadows, and waterfalls, around the place. And Nancy watched his fair, square face, his long, narrow nose, and his dark brows, from behind her thick eyelids.

"So you like Bombay enormously?" Farhat asked.

"O yes, I do. It has a lot of interesting things there. New films, beautiful evening programmes, young boys and girls, and a milling crowd of students. You know, I love crowd and movement. Even Delhi lacks the attraction that Bombay has. But still Delhi is better than this forest like place. I feel stifled here," said Nancy, fiddling with the radio knob.

She stayed her fingers on a pleasant and exciting orchestral music emitting from the radio. Music filled the air. Outside, it was drizzling. Farhat looked unblinkingly at Nancy, while she was lost in the waves of music.

"Do you like Indian films? I've a passion for them. More than the foreign ones. Their songs enter the heart, deep inside. You find your world, your own, familiar tunes. Interesting real-life stories unfold before your eyes."

"Well, I too love watching films. But our Indian movies have a very low artistic standard. Sometimes, even the techniques are ridiculous. In fact, I have noticed these oddities, these serious mistakes many times over. You are watching a royal *Mughal* court, and lo suddenly you discover a courtier there wearing white tennis shoes."

Nancy could not stop laughing at his description.

"That's true. I too have marked some telling discrepancies. In some movies scenes from the ancient past are shown with places beaming with electric lights. And then there are songs at every step."

"Oh don't talk about the songs. Our movies are little more than song sequences. I remember I went to see a film with my friend, once. It was '*Shireen Farhad* '. In a scene, *Shireen* fainted on learning about *Farhad's* death. I couldn't help exclaiming, '*Poor girl, she's going to die*!' My friend remarked instantly, '*She'll die only after singing a mournful song*.' These film makers make fun of human nature"

"Well, yes! They dress their women beggars in decent dresses, and instead of begging at daytime in the streets, these women are shown singing imploringly in the loneliness of lush gardens under soft moonlight."

"Wow, you are a very shrewd observer! But a few moments ago you were praising Indian films!"

"I don't care about the technical weaknesses. What attracts me is the suspense, the excitement in Indian movies. The romance there has an intensely personal touch, and their songs are so sweet and mellifluous! They fascinated me so much that I learnt a fair level of Urdu in my four years at college, though I had very little knowledge of it in my childhood. Our films carry us to strange but pleasant romantic dreamlands. They show life taken over by the deceptions of romance. Indeed, when realities become unpleasant, these colourful deceptions are the only springs of life." Nancy reflected ruefully, flicking her head in a coquettish fashion, lying back in her Victoria chair, her laden eyes half-open.

"Why don't you join films? Your height, your slender figure, attractive features, penetrating eyes, and your education and culture, are convincing proofs of your success." Farhat suggested with lively sincerity.

"Do you really think that—? But our movie idols are all run of the mill kind of fellows, demonstrating extravagant tastes." Nancy stopped saying something.

Her laden eyes displayed a quiet desperation. She quickly shrank back under the veil of modesty. The rain had stopped outside, but dark clouds were still shrouding the sky. The darkness of evening had embraced the landscape, save on the streets where pale light from the lamp posts was struggling for survival.

"Oho, I have to leave for a meeting. I'm going to deliver a speech. It's already seven now. I've only half hour to reach there!" Farhat suddenly recalled.

"You must be living a wonderful life, Mr. Farhat! Writing, lecturing, tours, amusements! And me! I've to spend my two long months in this prison house." Nancy spoke in a very sorrowful tone.

"Why don't you come down from this lofty plain? My humble house is ready to welcome you. Stay for at least two months with me. You'll have no problems there. I assure you. My town is brighter than yours. You'll find lots of college going students there. You can easily travel with me. I'm sure Dr. Santanam will allow you to stay with me. I've ample space in my house to welcome you."

"O, come on! I'm not going to take all your space. But, do you really mean it?"

"Look now, I've yet to sign this letter," said Farhat skirting her query away, and signing his letter, "Bye, bye then! I'm sorry I can't come tomorrow morning. I've to attend another meeting with the local journalists. I can come in the evening, but what if I couldn't meet Dr. Santanam tomorrow too? I think I should better visit you a day after. It will be Sunday then, and I could see him, I suppose."

"Please try to come tomorrow evening, even if daddy isn't at home. You can at least wait for him here." Nancy replied with a smile.

Cute dimples became more conspicuous on her blushing cheeks, and the boredom hitherto hidden in her, again started stretching its limbs. Farhat got up with a quick jerk, and shaking her hands warmly, left the drawing rooming, wishing her a very good night.

References

1. The Chota Nagpur Plateau is a plateau in eastern India, which covers much of Jharkhand state as well as adjacent parts of Orissa, West Bengal, Bihar and Chhattisgarh.
2. The upper edge of a sari that is wrapped on shoulders and the chest.
3. Puna is a town
4. The eyes of Hindu gods and goddesses at the Ajanta Caves in Aurangabad district of Maharashtra, India. The caves include paintings and sculptures considered to be masterpieces of Buddhist religious art as well as frescos reminiscent of the *Sigiriya* paintings in Sri Lanka.
5. '*Shireen Farhad*'

4. SADHU[1]

Sohail Azimabadi

There was once a small hut on the bank of a river, very far from the village. A sadhu *maharaj*[2] had been living in the hut for quite a long time. It was surrounded by a forest of brilliantly coloured flowers. In my childhood, I often went there to pluck flowers, and sometimes visited the sadhu's hut to ask for *prasad*[3]. I always found a crowd of devout followers of the sadhu in front of his hut. But no one knew anything in detail about the facts of his life.

Often in the stillness of the night, when the villagers drifted into sweet, restful sweep, the echoing cry of '*Harey Ram, Harey Ram*[4]' rent the still air, robbing the atmosphere of its calm. The incessant chant of the sadhu, on his nocturnal round of the village at the dead of night, frightened me whenever it broke my sleep.

I had seen other sadhus too in my childhood days, and even now I see no dearth of them begging like ordinary beggars in the narrow streets and lanes. But *maharaj* has never been spotted begging for alms or anything for that matter. Far from asking for charity, he never ever accepted any. A landlord, albeit, had fixed the revenue from about three acres of his agricultural land for the *sadhu*. The daily expenses of *maharaj* were met with the money from that land.

Maharaj had a lovely parrot. With its ritual chants of '*Harey Ram, Harey Ram*' every morning, this amazing bird attracted bathers going to the holy river to take their pre-breakfast bath. *Maharaj* was very fond of this parrot.

Amazing stories about *maharaj* were rife among his followers. Some said that he was seen flying like birds, during the dark, moonless nights, while others said that every part of his body split up and worshipped God separately. There were the others who said that he often stood for the whole night in the river, as an act of religious penance. And then the glorious light that exuded from his face, brilliantly illuminated the dark night to a distance. In fact there were many mouths of village gossip going around the place about him. But there was not a soul who really knew who the *maharaj* actually was.

The day when I came back home after taking my BA exams, my uncle took me to *sadhu maharaj*. He had a firm belief that the sadhu's one close look at me would bring me good fortune. But I had little faith in paranormal beliefs, though I never attacked them in public. However, my uncle's constant insistence forced me to accompany him to the sadhu.

As I was conveyed to the presence of the holy man, our eyes locked together, and I felt a sudden shiver running through my body. My lips lost their quiver and I lost my speech. I still remember those piercing red eyes! They looked like those of a drunkard. Long dishevelled hair, flowing unkempt beard, and bushy moustache, all combined to make his face appear so glorious and divine!

I was so lost in thoughts that I could not hear what transpired between him and my uncle. I asked myself why I got so quickly impressed by the man, whereas in fact I had no faith in a sadhu, whether the one before me or anybody else. But I didn't know what power radiated from the holy man that was slowly overpowering my soul. I was bathed in sweat. The spell was broken when the *maharaj* moved his lips, asking me to leave and also reminding me to visit him sometimes.

My encounter with that incredibly strange man instilled some kind of belief in him, and therefore I started visiting him everyday. I gradually gathered courage to converse with him, and was able to talk freely with him on various problems. It was amazing to find the *maharaj* talking about world history and the growth of materialism in the contemporary world. It clearly showed that the man possessed extensive knowledge. There was apparently nothing in his aspect to show that he was a man of such vast knowledge. I used to watch him dumbfounded when he spoke.

Misunderstandings about me cropped up in people's mind when they saw me so influenced by the man. My mother was so worried that she expressed openly about her fear of my conversion into a sadhu.

She openly cried in despair, "Oh, no! I'm so afraid my Manohar is going to become a sadhu!"

I tried to convince her that her fears were baseless, but she always asked me not to go there, and finding me adamant, one day she herself sent a message to the *maharaj* requesting him to prevent me from even thinking about becoming a sadhu, little knowing that in fact I never intended to be one.

One day, when I appeared before the *maharaj*, he said, "Manohar, it is better if you stop coming to me! Of course, it pains me a lot to ask you to do that. But, please don't come from now!"

Surprised at the sadhu's suggestion, I asked him, "Why *maharaj*! Forgive me, if I have committed any mistake. I touch your feet and apologize, but please don't send me away!"

"No, no Manohar, you haven't done anything wrong. Listen, your people think that you will become a sadhu under my influence, and they don't like it! So, I feel you shouldn't come here." The sadhu's voice was laced with affection.

I replied respectfully, "*Maharaj*, it's quite true that some people are nursing misunderstandings. In truth, I never thought of turning into a sadhu, and what's bad even if I did?"

The sadhu's eyes sparkled. He surveyed me with an intent gaze, and answered, "Manohar, if it's not a bad idea to live like a sadhu, it's not also a very noble idea. And it's a sin to turn a promising man like you into a sadhu. I hold the belief that to become a sadhu in youth is a sin and in old age an obligation. As you grow old your mind automatically finds refuge in '*yog*', in the philosophy and practice of abstinence, self-discipline, and sobriety."

A question slipped out of my mouth quite unwittingly, "*Maharaj*, what made you become an ascetic at an early age?"

The sadhu's radiant face suddenly darkened, as when clouds obscure the bright moonlight. He looked up at me very closely. Tears were glistening in his eyes.

"My dear Manohar, you've asked me a strange question, the answer of which I'd always avoided, to you even. But I'd not like you to harm yourself by even thinking of becoming an ascetic and, therefore, to clear your misunderstandings, listen carefully to what I am going to say now.

The world, my son, is so full of grand, seductive illusions that we cannot easily turn our faces away. The more we try to run away from it, the faster we are trapped in the fascinating web of its deception. I know many of those who have become sadhus, have done so for a living. And the world indiscreetly issues them the credentials of self-denying hermits. The rest become sadhus because that is perhaps the only escape route for them.

There are others who become sadhus only after family break-ups. Besides, many notorious criminal and murderers have assumed the garb of a sadhu, for fear of being exposed to the world. No doubt, there are still people whose deep religious devotion has inspired them to take to asceticism. But I don't grant any importance to them. Much more respectful than them, in my eyes, is the family man who leads a very pious life together with his wife and children. To run away from worldly responsibilities for fear of sin is the ultimate proof of weakness. Think it long and hard, and tell me whom would you revere, the man who dives into the river and swims across successfully to the other side, or the one who stares out to the river from a distance and refuses to swim for fear of drowning.

Well, I'm now going to tell you the sad story of my life, and the incident that compelled me to become a sadhu. When you consider it deeply, you may come to the conclusion that I've done a wonderful job. But actually I've there's nothing marvellous in it. You'll clearly notice how helpless I was in opting for the life of a hermit. If on the one hand I've chosen to live a life of self-denial and abstinence as atonement for my sins, on the other hand, I'm also guilty of the sin of shirking away from my duties towards my wife and children."

The *maharaj* fell silent for some time. I found myself in a rather strange situation, and gazed at him in surprise. His speech sent currents flowing through my mind, and sparks flaring inside my body.

After a pause, the *maharaj* looked quizzically at me, and spoke, "Listen! I was born into a wealth Brahmin family, the only child of my parents. I had an aunt who became a childless widow a few months after her marriage. After her husband's death she came to live with us in our house. I was brought with great love and care, and over the years my aunt had grown immensely fond of me. If my father punished me for my childish pranks, she would cry her eyes out. When this sequential drama became everyday affair, she took me to her house in Allahabad, and put me in a school. I was ten years old at then.

My aunt had a maidservant called Rohni, from the *kahar* family. She was a widow and had a daughter called Mohni. When I came to Allahabad, Mohni must be around four years old and was a very cute little child. I loved her immensely but innocently, as children do in their tender age. We grew up together, and when she was seven years old, Mohni in accordance with the village tradition, was married to a village boy, but was not sent to live with her husband because of her young age, and stayed with us.

And to be quite honest with you Mohan, I could not hold my sly, guilty looks falling on her as she started growing. An overwhelming desire arose in my mind and occupied its permanent seat there. In fact, I never tried to drive it away from its resting place. On the contrary, it flourished there to the extent that, often when I was alone, I enjoyed playing with it in my imagination with Mohni as my playmate.

Years rolled on, and I, now a young man of twenty, was doing my MA. Mohni was still living with us. I was exceptionally intelligent and popular, and so offers for my marriage started pouring in from eager parents of marriageable daughters. My youth, quite naturally, carried with it all its spirited dalliance and reckless expenditure of feeling. Mohni had also grown up, and spring had dawned on her with a hush admiring its own image in her beautiful bloom. The shivering pulsation of youth in me was restless for her embrace.

One day, my aunt and her maid Rohini went to attend a marriage ceremony of one of our relatives. I too had gone with them, but came back early, immediately after dinner. It was approaching midnight when I reached home. The guard at the gate was drowsing, and the gate was closed. I thought my aunt had also come back, so I called out and knocked at the door. To my surprise, I found Mohini opening the door for me.

Her disheveled appearance, looking as though she had just fallen out of bed, her sleepy eyes, her tousled hair, and her rumpled clothes, all made me delirious like a drunkard. Controlling my emotions from spilling over, I asked her if my aunt had come back. She said nothing and I headed straight to my room. I climbed to my bed with an intensely powerful feeling welling up inside me. *Why, for fear of my aunt, had I been avoiding talking to her, not even throwing her a smile?* That night the fear was not present. Burning, amorous desires fuelled for their fulfillment, and baser emotions craved for their expression, as I called her out to bring me a glass of water. After a few moments, she entered the room with the glass in her hand. I looked at her anxiously as a thief who was caught red-handed, and quite lost in her seductive form, forgot to shift my gaze. The moment she turned round to leave, after putting the glass on the table, I caught her hand and felt it tremble in my warm clasp. She tried to break free from my clench, but gave in against its sheer power, protesting in a hushed voice, '*Oh, no! What are you doing? I will tell bibiji*[6]". Her threatening words immediately brought me to my senses, and trembling, for fear of disgrace and insult, I left her hand free.

But the unquenched desires fuelling inside me refused to die down. I picked up a knife lying on the table, and spoke out, '*Look Mohini! I can't live without you. I had been burning in your love for quite some time, and if you reject me like this, I'm going to take my own life.*' I drew the knife closer to my chest, and as I was going to thrust it in, she caught my hand and said,

'*Please don't do it*!' My rebellious feelings got a new lease of life, and I uttered them, '*It's really useless for me to live without you, and you can't always stop me from dying*!' How weak is a woman's heart, how credulous her mind! How easily she can be won by even a feigned expression of love! Mohini held me in a warm embrace."

The *sadhu* could not continue his story and began trembling. He was looking like the innocent person who had been wrongly convicted of an appalling crime. He wept openly for a while, and then wiping his tears, continued, "Careless of its consequences, I enjoyed playing with her blooming youth for about three months. During that period my marriage also got fixed, and I went back to my village home. This was the time of my life when I was always ready to commit a sin whenever my eyes fell on any fair damsel.

After some time Mohini and my aunt also came to live with us. One day when there was no one at home, Mohini came to my room and broke the news that she had become pregnant. She asked me to take her to Allahabad anyhow, and get her pregnancy terminated or else she would not be able to survive in the society. I got angry at her courage, as she was no more an object of interest for me, and dismissed her, rebuking her sharply. But the thought of an impending infamy made me restless. The thought how the act of sin steals peace away from a man's life, kept me worrying. I maintained, nevertheless, a grave silence suppressing the tumultuous storm rising inside.

We woke up the next morning to discover that there was no trace of Mohini in the house. We searched far and wide but she was not to be found. People were distressed at the incident, and her mother cried uncontrollably. Everyone at home was stunned with pain and awe, only I stayed unaffected and composed. Rumours about her went flying around. I knew the reason of her disappearance, and was relieved she had gone away. My fear had vanished, and I was free now. Isn't it strange, Manohar, how after committing a sin man becomes extremely remorseless and heard-hearted!

Weeks, months, and years went by and Mohini was not to be found. I was now a married man with two children. Rohini died crying in grief for her daughter. But I never regretted my deed, nor did my conscience reproach me. My lust for the pleasures of the flesh grew unabated, and my outrageous desires remained unquenched. Righteous, positive thoughts never crossed my mind. I don't know how many blooming flowers I had crushed, and snatched their charm in the desert of my burning desire, earning their curses.

It was roughly sixteen years back that I went on a tour to *Benares*[7]. One day, as I was coming out of water after taking a bath in the Ganges, I saw a woman passing by my side on the river bank. She threw a piercing glance at me and went away. She was a middle aged woman and was wearing a very expensive dress. Her face hadn't yet completely lost the splendour of youth.

The next day when I again went to the river bank, a man came to me and told me that the '*bai*'[8] was waiting for me. I asked him to come back in the evening and take me there, as I wasn't familiar with the way. There was no name in the letter, but I gathered from it that it was from a prostitute. I wasn't surprised, since I already knew many of them.

The man appeared in the evening and took me to the place. The woman whom I had seen on the river bank welcomed me at the door of a decorated house, and took me inside. I tried hard but could not recognize her, and when she discovered my perplexed face, she spoke out, '*Ramesh babu, haven't you recognized me?*' Deeply embarrassed, I could only say, '*Not, really! I'm sorry!*' She said, '*Oh, yes! Why should you know me now? Listen, I'm the same Mohini whom you have devastated.*' I suddenly felt as if thunder had shaken the ground under my feet. My head hung in shame. I fell utterly silent, and watched a young, beautiful girl entering the room. Mohini said to the girl, '*Mona, touch his feet! He is your father, darling!*' The girl touched my feet and saluted me, sitting in front, looking at me with love and respect. Heaven seemed falling on me. I was dumbfounded and stunned.

It's very difficult for me to narrate to you how I felt at that moment. Things were whirling before my eyes. Someone was hitting me from my inside, my whole body convulsed and I cried within. Mohini, finding me unable to speak, urged, '*Speak, Ramesh babu! Why are you silent now?*' But how could I speak? I was a sinner before her and the burden of guilt didn't allow me to lift my head or move my lips.

She continued when I refused to utter a word, '*One has to receive punishment for his sins, anyway, anyhow. I forgot my duties, and the love that was someone else's trust on me, I surrendered to you. I'm still suffering the punishment, living the wretched life of a disgraced prostitute, and though born and brought in a family house, will die as a prostitute. You outraged my modesty, destroyed my life and threw me out, and see how you are punished for your sins. Your own daughter is living the life of a prostitute with me.*'

I could not hear all that Mohini was saying, boiling with emotions, and unable to hear more, I silently got up and left the place. What I had seen and heard was enough to drown me with shame and regret. I had no other option after all that had happened with me, except accepting the punishment of shunning the world altogether, following complete abstinence from all worldly pleasures, and leading the life of a sadhu, for my expiation, my deliverance."

The hut is a desolate place now. The sadhu suddenly vanished one night, leaving the place in darkness. People say the sadhu had taken *Samadhi*, submitting to be buried alive. But his name still lives on the tongues of the inhabitants of Yashanpur village.

I still yearn to listen to the voice of sadhu *maharaj*.

References

1. a Hindu holy man, especially one who lives away from people and society.
2. a respectful term for a Brahmin guru.
3. offerings that a Hindu makes to a Hindu deity.
4. the Hindu chant of their deity *Ram*
5. a lower caste of Hindus known, whose business was to carry palanquins, or do domestic chores.
6. respectful term for the mistress of the house.
7. a town in north India in the state of Uttar Pradesh.
8. prostitute

5. SHADES OF PAIN

Mohammed Mohsin

"Mummy, look Sundri *didi* has again dropped the metal pot and dented it!" Rajni complained as she came running to her mother.

"Send that blasted girl to me! She's going to ruin my house."

In fact, it was not Sundri's fault. She was just walking back from the nearby water well after washing the dishes, carrying them, one upon the other, on her head. Rajni was also with her. As Sundri was plodding down the way, her stole slipped from her shoulders and one end of it touched the ground. She quickly caught the other end and held it up by drawing her hand down from the position where she was balancing the dishes. In the midst of this shaking and moving, the pot sitting at the top fell down bumping on the ground.

Sundri was harshly punished by her aunt that day, more because of Rajni's constant groans and gripes about her than for her own fault.

Sundri was six years old when she was left in charge of her aunt by her dying mother. She had been living with her aunt since then. This woman already had a few of her own children. And there was no reason why she would accept an added burden without being compensated. So Sundri had to wash her cousins' clothes, clean their dishes, and bear their chidings and tantrums. In return for these services, she was given two meals every day. A slight mistake in performance of her duties forced her to suffer not only rebukes and beatings, but also starvation.

The neighbours said that Sundri was beautiful like a rose. But her aunt didn't like to hear that. She always recounted her weaknesses contrasting them with Rajni's stainless manners, her innocence, and her attractive face. She felt people were kind to Sundri partly because they pitied her as an orphan, and partly because they were jealous of Rajni. Penniless Sundri had nothing to arouse people's envy. The more Sundri's aunt thought about her the more she hated her. She had decided to take revenge from Sundri for what she considered as her neighbours' injustices to her own daughter. So she started deliberately picking faults with everything that she did, and gratified herself by punishing her. The severest punishment for Sundri was to starve her. Her aunt gave her nothing to eat for the whole day. And this, in fact, was the toughest test that Sundri had to suffer. As for the usual daily smacks and rebukes, she looked for them the way one does for the rays of the sun every morning. Not a day passed when she didn't have to welcome curses, invectives, and even slaps. They were now as clichéd to her as those morning rays.

Sometimes, these rebukes and spanks came to Sundri as bearers of glad tidings, as the elixirs of life. She awaited them restlessly, as it were, with a longing heart, whenever she committed a mistake. But she dreaded when her aunt's wrath flared beyond limits, because then it immobilized her hands and tongue, and she quietly deprived Sundri of any food for the whole day. Blood drained from Sundri's body at the thought of starvation—the abject misery of being deprived of full two meals! She had a sinking feeling in the pit of her stomach watching the entire household eating their belly full right in front of her, and the poor girl, serving them their food, watching them eat with delight, clearing the table, washing their dishes, and helplessly looking at the leftovers being given to the dogs and cats. Sundri had to douse the fire of hunger raging in her stomach with glasses of water only. She trembled with fear at the thought of such a punishment. What if her aunt beat her savagely, she at least gave her the leftover to eat! Sundri couldn't help making those unavoidable little mistakes that were bound to happen everyday. She paid for them fittingly, willingly, carefully avoiding the big ones. The abuses and battering, in any case, guaranteed her food, without which she would be shattered.

Chaco, Sundri's cousin, was the only son in the house. He was raised so indiscreetly that he grew up to become a reckless vagabond like a stray street dog. At home, nobody dared to go against his wishes. He would hit anybody he liked. Not a soul could complain if he snatched food out of anyone's mouth. Sundri was the softest target of his raving brutality. But Sundri couldn't even dare to open her mouth. The other children, on the other hand, were allowed to grumble at Chaco's indecencies, and her aunt would just frown slightly at her son.

Apart from other numerous services, Sundri also had to rub Chaco's legs after dinner, every evening. Persistent sharp pinches and countless abuses woke her up the moment she slipped into doze while doing the job.

It was one of those nights when Sundri was doing her post dinner chore. Everyone in the house was sleeping. But Chaco was still awake, and Sundri had to keep rubbing his legs till he drifted into sleep. Once, while in the midst of performing her duty, Sundri fell into a drowse, and hit the floor with a dull thud. Chaco who himself had dozed off, was woken up by the sound. He got up with a sudden start, and catching her hand started twisting it, and pinched hard on her arm. Sundri rolled in pain, but Chaco didn't care to stop, and kicked her so hard that she fell flat on the ground. With an intensely passionate look he cast his eyes on Sundri's dishevelled body. The dim light of the lantern informed him of her blooming youth for the first time. Fuelled by a fiercely carnal desire, he pounced on her like a hungry animal. Sundri struggled desperately to get away, but Chaco's powerful arms held her tight in their iron clutch. Her bones creaked under the enormous pressure of his grasp. Sundri became powerless. Chaco's lust had at once introduced her to the contrasting experiences of despair and pleasure. Chaco continued his night attacks on Sundri with the same force and ferocity.

Sundri was now fully grown up, but her aunt never thought of finding a suitable match for her. Perhaps the compelling need of Sundri's services didn't allow her to think about her marriage. When quizzed by her neighbours, she would evasively say, "Oh, I'm so worried about it. You know, I spend sleepless nights thinking about finding a mate for her. But what can I do? Nobody asks for her hand in marriage. And we are from the girl's side, we can't send marriage proposals."

But it gradually dawned on the neighbours that Sundri's aunt wanted her to just stay at home and do the household chores. Women in the vicinity accosted Sundri's aunt in the streets, taunting her, "Stop fooling us, Chaco's mother! We know you aren't bothered about her; she isn't your own daughter. You've got a maid servant for free. You're worried who'd look after your house if she's married away, aren't you?"

She knew nobody could force her to get Sundri married. It was not a police case, so she wasn't afraid of them either. And above all, Sundri was her niece, her own responsibility; strangers had anything to do with their relationship. Sundri was not living on their food. So, Sundri's aunt turned a deaf ear to all taunts and complaints. Besides, she knew it well that nobody would agree to marry a destitute like Sundri. She herself was not ready to bear her marriage expenses. And then, her daughter herself was still single. The thought of getting her daughter married occupied her mind more than anything else. She had kept safe whatever little was there in the house for her dowry.

And then one day she received a marriage proposal for Sundri. When the boy's parents asked her about the dowry, she told them clearly, "I'm not going to pay a single penny. I've raised her single-handedly with whatever money I could manage. Do you want me to sell my house now and start begging?"

The marriage proposal was finally turned down by the boy's family because they considered it an insult to bring a daughter-in-law without any jewels on her. There was no other proposal after that. But the onslaught of the neighbours' grilling was increasing by the day. Chaco's mother was fed up with providing clarifications. Until one day, she silently fixed Sundri's marriage with a man from a neighbouring village. Jamai, the suitor, was a widower and a habitual drunkard. He had had a large farm, but had wasted all on drinking. Now working on a petty salary in a printing house, he spent most of what he earned on his lust for liquor.

Jamai married Sundri and brought her home. But this important change in her status did not affect her life. She had to do the same household jobs, cleaning the dishes, stoking up fire in the clay oven, rubbing Jamai's body till late night, and welcoming his kicks and abuses in return. He always returned home blind drunk, and played violently with her body, reminding her of Chako's oppressions. She mustered her maximum strength in defending herself against Jamai's savage attacks also, but gave away helplessly, as usual, overpowered ultimately, by the familiar experiences of joy and trauma.

One night, while Jamai was returning home dead drunk, he tripped on the loose stones and was seriously hurt in the head. He fell into a coma and died after a few days.

Unforeseen problems cropped up in Sundri's life after Jamai's death. Continuous starvation had left her almost emaciated. An ominous, shroud-like gloom deepened on her bloodless white cheeks. Her once luminous eyes lost their lustre, and dark curves formed around them, like poverty peering from the cracks of ruins. Sundri would have never found deliverance from her miserable life hadn't Mensa, a friendly woman in the neighbourhood with some connections, taken her to Bombay and introduced her to a new world.

Sundri was now breathing in a world where a young woman's beauty and physical charm no more made her a hapless and helpless prey to men's lust and piercing looks. She had reached a place where, from her wealth and beauty, she could change the destiny of men, like bright, colourful mountain flowers hitherto ignored and trampled, upon reaching the golden vases, become precious and prized possessions.

Blessed with fate, Sundri was traversing through strange paths in her new world. A treasure had emerged from under the deserted waste land. Accomplished classical singers, discovering a natural musicality in her voice, successfully trained her in the art of singing, and the magnetic charm of her songs started attracting the wealth of people in high places and palaces in Bombay. Very soon, Sundri's name and fame reached the Bombay film industry, and a famous film company signed her for a lead cast in their film.

In a very short time, Sundri became a well-known actress. Her artistically carved face, the disarming elegance of her rich-brown complexion, the perfect and pleasing symmetry between the members of her body, her enchanting and wondrous mannerisms, her soft, lute-like voice, and to top it all, her superb acting, all combined to make her a phenomenon rarely to be found in a single actor. When she appeared on the big screen she looked like a masterpiece of creation, as if imagination had been moulded into flesh and skin. Nobody knew her as Sundri in the film world. She was now famous as Indira Devi, the heart throb of the country, with whom everybody craved to talk.

The depraved luckless gewgaw of society was transformed into a glamorous celebrity. Before she stepped into the film world, she was an attraction for the licentious nobles and uncivilized businessmen only. But now a few moments of her company were considered to be a matter of pride by even the most successful and dignified people. When she visited a new town or city, the huge crowd of spectators thronged her like the storm of insects around the electric lamps on the roads. Fan mails kept pouring into her mailbox. Cleopatra's traditional figure was sketched on the canvass of words and proven inferior to her beauty. Her voice was considered a miracle, her inimitable acting the envy of those masters of the art who were worshipped as gods. She had learnt to read and write after entering the film world, so she understood the sense and importance of being known as a '*star*', the '*one and only one*' or an '*idol*'—words that she found in her fan letters. She, however, was so tired of their abundance and monotony that she consigned them to the dustbins. Some letters sounded incredibly romantic, but they hardly struck any chord in her.

People in high places came to pay her a visit and praised her beauty and exceptional talent. There were those who expressed their readiness to sacrifice all on the altar of her beauty. Sundri, on the contrary, was never moved by their innocent open avowals. They were surprised to discover that the enchanting beauty, who danced like lightning on the stage, appeared so lifeless and dull to their romantic overtures. All their renewed efforts to stimulate romantic emotions in her came a cropper. Realizing that they had offended Sundri by their loose talks, they would stop talking. And the silence from both sides made the entire atmosphere heavy, forcing them to leave. They didn't dare to ask Sundri why she was indifferent to them. In a short space of time, rumours about Sundri's typical behaviour spread far and wide. Her frigid personal life and her lacklustre approach appeared puzzling to her fans.

After signing a new contract with another film company, Sundri shifted to Calcutta. The company's manager had signed Sundri after putting in a great deal of effort, and winning the consent of a great star like her apparently meant that the man had rendered an outstanding service to his company. But the truth was that he was burning with an all-consuming love for Sundri. He cared little about bringing glory to the company, and was driven by a craving for her love and attention. He consistently tried to draw closer to Sundri, but could not express his feelings to her because of her influential position and popularity.

He invited her, her alone, on dinner one night, because he wished to keep the meeting a private affair. An excellent dinner was laid out on the lawn. Sundri and the manager sat opposite each other. Bright moonlight had cast a silvery net on the atmosphere. The rambling early April air was arousing a feeling of ecstasy.

The manager was overcome with strong emotion. The raging storm of a longing desire had accelerated his heartbeats. He talked leisurely during the dinner, but could not dare to open his heart to her. Sundri's enchanting beauty betrayed a seductive charm by the moonlight.

Gazing her in awe, the manager at last opened his mouth, "Would you permit me to say something, Indira Devi?"

"Oh sure, please feel free!" She replied.

"If you don't mind . . ." the manager spoke faltering, "I first saw you in the film, "*The New Bride*", and I was mesmerised by your exceptional good looks. The fact is that you don't look half as beautiful in your films as you do in real life. Our company's extremely lucky to have you with us, and I particularly . . .", he stopped without completing the sentence, looked at Sundri, and finding no expression on her face, felt embarrassed.

"Why did you stop? You were going to say something about yourself!" Sundri asked him sincerely.

"My frankness would probably displease you!"

"Come on, express yourself!" Sundri looked visibly annoyed.

"I was all yours the day I saw your picture. And since then I've been looking forward to winning your favour through the power of my love. Indira Devi, I'm ready to sacrifice all for you!" there was passion in the manager's tone.

Sundri appeared coldly indifferent to the man's avowals of love.

"Wouldn't you consider my request, Sundri Devi?" The man asked, casting an imploring look at her.

Baffled at her absolute silence, the man drew his chair closer beside Sundri. Something inside her, perhaps the memories of her utter helplessness against blatant force, compelled her, and she, quite unwittingly, leaned sideways, bending her naked shoulders close to the manager.

"Why don't you respond, Sundri Devi?" the man was restless now.

And again she refrained from uttering a word. She looked demoralized and powerless, like a boy waiting for his teacher's inevitable chastisement. Her eyelids had drooped and her breath was slowing down. This puzzled the manager greatly. What he expected was that the Sundri, who scuttled on the stage like lightning, would respond to her request in a romantic vein. He feared he might be sounding unpleasant to her, but burning with passionate desire, he could not control himself and turned towards her.

"Sundri Devi . . . !" his voice was quivering with passion.

Sundri lifted her eyes. They looked blistering with fire, as when someone is furious and vexed at his compelling helplessness. The manager was bewildered and confused. Sundri's gaze rested on the manager, apparently waiting for his next step. Not having the guts to meet her eyes, the man looked down to the ground. And suddenly a hard resounding slap struck across his face. Sundri's unexpected wrath and its equally unexpected reaction frightened the manager.

Finding himself weak enough to lift his eyes, he stumbled over his words, "So s . . . s . . . sorry . . . Sundri Devi! Please forgive me. I misunderstood you."

Regret and shame writ large and clear on his face. Sundri jumped up from her chair, and gripping the corner of the tablecloth pulled it with a jerk. She was breathing heavily with anger. The plates and all that was on the table cover fell to the floor, breaking into tiny pieces. Terrified, the manager shrunk into his chair. Sundri turned her eyes to him. In addition to anger those eyes now carried a request, an entreaty. Miserably confounded, the manager sat glued to his chair. Knocking the chairs over, taking quick, long, jerky steps, Sundri walked out of the manager's house.

6. THE DEEP RED SHARD OF GLASS

Kalam Haidari

Why Sushil, what are you thinking, now? Why are you looking so hopelessly lost? What's this madness? What for are you staring at that broken grape-coloured piece of glass? What's so important in that? It looks so weird and jagged!

Look now! Your eyes are so glued to the broken glass piece that you have even failed to notice your appointment letter from Shankar Jain & Modi[1] *has fluttered to the floor. Aren't you happy at that wonderful piece of news?*

Perhaps the reddish tint of that shard has held your rapt attention. Is that the reason why you have wasted not less than forty minutes holding it in your palm, looking at it so patiently?

You're so careless about everything else in your room. Your study table has lost one of its legs. And one of the bricks that you have piled there, for support, is slipping out, and others too appear to follow suit, closely, suddenly.

And, what's that empty can of beer doing there, sitting on your table for so many days?

I'm afraid the broken glass may hurt you, if you keep on holding it in your palm for long. It has dangerously scalloped edges! You'll soil your hands. Its edges are covered with thick dry mud!

But oh, no! Sushil . . . young man . . . , where have you vanished now?

O, I can see you now, washing that glass fragment! But why are you doing that? Be careful, it may cut your fingers.

I can read your thoughts drifting back to the air conditioned office at Shankar Jain & Modi, and to that pretty office secretary. Is she in any way associated with that glass piece? She's still single, perhaps. I remember, her shapely breasts had puffed out so challengingly that you almost . . .

Weren't you staring at her breasts that day when she was informing the Assistant Manager on phone about your arrival? Don't stare like that, my dear boy! It's an affront to public decency. I've always reprimanded you for that. Aren't you aware of my presence? Of course, I'm here, watching you close by. You are wrong to think I have walked out on you.

I'm very much here, young man, always by your side, watching you, talking to you!

Throw away that splintered glass, young man! I warn you again. You will cut your fingers. Don't you see, it's broken and has very rough, sharp edges? Its sides are so pointed! They can prick your skin.

The house that fronts mine lies abandoned. Its occupants had left it some while ago. The panes of its front windows had fallen off fragmenting into small pieces, one of which has of late become *Sushil's* most valued possession or obsession. That fateful day when the windowpanes were shattered was the day when all that defines humanity was broken into smithereens. Glasses, anyway, have to break. They are more fragile. But these glasses were smashed to pieces very ruthlessly.

Look now, your appointment letter has fallen on the floor and landed near the shoes you had bought in Bombay! I watched you looking intently at the stunningly beautiful, sprightly, young girl who was arguing with the salesman at the shoe store. Weren't you looking down salaciously at the lower part of her body, below her waist? Your eyes sliding up and down her shapely frame, I watched them navigating through her every twist and turn.

The colour of the window pane in her room was also deep red. Passing through her house, on your usual evening wanderings didn't you sometimes feel as if a pair of eyes was staring at you from behind that pane? But you are silly, Sushil! How did you see her eyes? You must have had visions. Don't you know you can't see anything through those tinted glass panes? They are used in windows for that very reason, my dear fellow.

The girl seemed to have an everlasting impression in your mind. You carried her in your mind wherever you went. You looked so lost. Didn't your thought drift back to her, when the Assistant Manager at Shankar Jain & Modi asked you to submit your application on a prescribed form? She must have silently crept into your mind while you were collecting your form at the counter.

You took the form and turned away quickly without saying thank you to the girl at the counter! You then got into a bus regretting your impoliteness all through the way back home. Didn't you? Lost in your thoughts, you perhaps failed to notice that the Sardarji[2] seated a couple of rows back had caught a pickpocket in action, and started beating him, with the other passengers wilfully participating in the activity, landing their shares of punches and blows on the poor fellow's face. Impervious to the ruckus around, all that while, I think, you were very busy fretting over your rudeness to that girl.

Look, how the light puff of wind has blown the piece of paper off your shoes, and it has now landed squarely on the empty suitcase lying worn out and chapped, in a far corner of the room, hoping for the day, when its belly would be stuffed!

January 2 . . .

. . . I haven't stepped out of my house for fear of the curfew. The town has become exceedingly dangerous. It appears governance and rule of law have taken a long holiday. Only last evening, a rioting mob of probably one thousand hooligans attacked our small *mahalla*[3], targeting the *Muslim* family living in the house facing mine. I closed my doors and windows, when I saw that the baying rabble had entered that house.

"Hey . . . hey . . . come along, guys! Kill them, all!"

"Yeh . . . yeh . . . quick . . . finish 'em off!"

Frantic shouts, heart-rending screams, agonizing cries, and the maddening sound and fury went on for almost an hour. The sound of the breaking of doors and panes, and of the kicking and pounding of feet, continued unabated. The police arrived late at night, when the appalling blood-game had ended, and the whole *mahalla*[3] lay wrapped in deathly silence, like an abandoned graveyard. The orgy had left the house in ruin, the doors were broken down, and empty boxes and torn clothes littered all around. An old woman was found dead on the veranda of the house, and the body of a young teenage boy lay in a pool of blood on the street. Their dead bodies were thrown on a heap of countless others stacked in a police truck.

I felt as if I were a corpse, helpless and frozen, and tumbled motionless on my bed like the heap of corpses in the truck.

January 6 . . .

The bloody communal riot was quelled at long last. It was discovered that the mad frenzy in the town erupted as a reaction of communal flare-ups in other parts of the country. The vicious chain of reactions set off by mob fury can hardly be brought under control, especially in a nation where the political system feeds on it.

I felt vaguely disturbed whenever my eyes fell on that empty house. I was told that the owner of the house who ran a fruit shop in Calcutta, had come back, and was rushing around madly in the house, as if still looking for some signs of life there.

His eighteen years old daughter was neither among the dead nor found amid the living. *Where then was she?* She must be somewhere, for sure, though hidden from his eyes. And her house stood empty and desolate. This was the house where for years, waking or in dream, she had heard the sonorous notes of *shehnai*[4], and echoes of mellow songs sung to the accompaniment of *dholak*[5], reverberating in her ears. Her dreamy eyes were filled with the vision of her dream hero, in the midst of the song and dance.

It was the same house where, flying on the viewless wings of her night-time fancies, she had dreamt of being carried away in a *doli*[6] to her bridegroom. She must have promised the henna plant in her courtyard, to decorate her hands with its dark red colour. The *henna*[7] plant had flowered for the bride, spreading its delicate branches, waiting to lend colour to her fingers. But her house and her dreams lay devastated, and she lost in a forlorn land.

My dear Sushil

You have left this place only six months ago, my son! But I'm after all your mother, and to me it appears as if it has been an age since I last saw you. I was terribly anxious when I heard that a Hindu-Muslim riot had broken out in your town. Hadn't I received your telegram on time, I would have set off to see you, caring less to be killed by any scoundrel on the way.

May God keep you safe and sound, my son! They say that many Muslims were killed in the riot, and a large number of those who remained, have left the town. *Surender Chowdhury*, the son of the village headman, was saying that there were too many Muslims in your town, and most of them had big businesses. They employed the Hindus and treated them very shabbily. He said that he felt like chomping him raw, whenever he caught sight of a Muslim. You know, he is an irascible fellow.

Usha sends her *pranam*[8] to you. We've to get her married soon. May *Ishwar* help and save you, my son! Keep writing to me regularly!'

Your mother!

The International Club was bustling with life. *Shri*[9] *Gopal Prasad Sanwarya*, the biggest government stockist of iron and steel, the proprietor of Great Standard Mercantile, and a close friend of the Minister of Industries, had hosted a dinner in honour of *Mr. Sohni*, ICS, the District Magistrate of the city, who was transferred, it was rumoured, because of the communal riot in the town. *Mr. Sohni* had joined as District Magistrate only a year ago.

The guests had started arriving from seven in the evening, though the dinner was scheduled at nine. The Club building was bathed in light from outside, and inside bright streams of light were bursting out in an arc, like a cascade.

Mr. Qadir Beg, the retired commissioner was bending on the velvety billiards table. His young daughter, clad in vibrant red *saree*[10], looking like a blazing flame, was standing in a corner, staring unblinkingly, at *Dr. Bhargava*, the History professor, who was standing in the front corner, talking to *Gopi Ram Didwania*, the cloth merchant, explaining to him that the *Taj Mahal*, in fact, was not built by the *Moghul Emperor Shahjahan*, but by a *Rajput King* . . .

"Hello, *Mr. Bhargava*!" *Safdar Arfi* suddenly entered the hall, and called out.

Dr. Bhargava didn't move an inch, but waved at him with a light smile, and continued his speech, "I was going to tell you *Mr. Didwania* that many other famous monuments, including the *Taj Mahal*, which are counted among the glorious architectural splendours built by Muslim kings, are in fact, monuments erected by our great builders. The truth is that, history written during *Mughal* reign had deliberately misrepresented the amazing accomplishments of the Hindu civilization, as the definitive proof of Muslim cultural superiority."

Didwania gave a huge yawn, and recalled that he had to deliver a dozen blankets, two bales of mercerized cotton, four pieces of *Binny's*[11] tere-cotton suiting, six pairs of bed covers, and . . .

"So *Mr. Didwania*, as long as the Hindu nation fails to realize how hundreds of years of slavery has deprived them of their glorious cultural heritage, there will be no revival of Hinduism, and . . ."

Didwania cut him short and said, "Excuse me, *Dr. Bhargava*, just wait a moment. I'll be back soon."

His eyes had fallen on the daughter of the Income tax Commissioner. She was entering the hall, with an air of coquetry, her *gharara*[12] billowing around her.

"Oho, you're alone, *Miss* . . . ! Where is *Mr. Gaur*?"

"Hi, uncle! *Papa*'s just close behind."

Didwania pulled a chair for her, but before she could allow her lissom frame to settle on it, *Mr. Sharan*, the young IAS officer, reached out to her, and holding her hand walked down to the arbour where perchance or purposely two folding steel chairs lay empty.

Glasses were raised and clinked, everybody wished everybody else, and sent the draughts of whisky trickling down their throats. Perhaps, *Safdar Arfi* had again recited a verse; the whole gathering was giving him a rapturous ovation.

Somebody, among the drunken frolickers, belched out, "You know *Achalji*, Urdu is nothing more than just a form of Hindi. It has to be accepted just like that—a mere variety of Hindi!"

Achalji, the recipient of that piece of information, started thinking on *Bhargava's* latest discovery, raising the glass of whisky to his lips!

"The fact is that this country of ours achieved freedom in 1947, from two slaveries."

Just then, they heard the screech of tyres. A car had just pulled in the portico.

The doors of the luxury sedan opened, and the middle-aged Deputy Chief Engineer emerged from it, with his two sons and five grown-up daughters, who mingled with the bubbling medley of men and women, like the colours of a rainbow spanning the sky.

"Very sorry for being late, gentlemen!"

"Hello, *Mr. Safdar Arfi*!" the plump, shapely daughter of the Engineer called out.

"At your service, miss!" *Safdar Arfi* was a picture of submission and humility.

Mr. Beg's stunningly beautiful daughter had at last found a quiet, lonely place for herself. She was drowned in thought, tilting back on a small tree in the garden, flanking the hall, from whose skylight thin beams of light were filtering out.

Sajjad, the clever son of the government advocate was discussing with *Mr. Sanwarya* on the issue of the flagging economic climate in the country, and the effects of devaluation. Remembering something, he suddenly turned around, and his eyes fell on *Mr. Beg's* daughter.

He rushed out, and approached her, "*Miss Beg*, why are you sitting here all alone, away from the jollity?"

"Oh, I'm just loosening up! What about yourself? When are you going to London?"

"I haven't yet decided, *Miss Beg*. In fact, I'm not really interested in going there. Events around have taken such a bizarre turn that it looks as if . . . Let's not talk any more about that *Miss Beg*!" Moved by her charm, loneliness, and monotony, *Sajjad* avoided entering into serious talks with her.

The clock on the wall of the Club said two by the night. Stray dogs were roaming the streets around the International Club.

The whole town lay in stillness, eerie and absolute.

O night, thou art the harbinger of peace, the haven of secrecy and tranquillity! Thou dost conceal and cover!

Sushil, now that you have returned after one full week, why do you look so astonished to see that the windows of the house in front are wearing new panes. And a large board on the outside of the house reads, 'The Islamic Relief Committee Office.

What are you searching in your travel bag, young man? You'll never get it, man. Do you remember where you've put it? What will you do with that broken piece of glass now? Look at the window of the facing house. It has adorned new panes on it. How beautiful are they! Their green colour has even turned the white lights inside appear green.

Your travel bag looks like that of a juggler's. It has so many pockets. Why are you rummaging through them all?

It is not there in the first pocket.

No, not too in the second pocket!

The third pocket is also empty.

And that small pocket with a zip?

Why? What's that? Now, how did you cut your fingers? Oho, it's that same shard of glass. It had to happen to you. Whoever touches it will face the same consequence. How dangerous are its edges?

I can see it now. It's the piece of glass from the broken windows of the house facing yours.

"We have distributed three hundred seventy-two blankets among the refugees. Seventeen thousand three hundred sixty-two rupees eighty-seven paisa have been spent on feeding them. Twenty-five families have been rehabilitated. Seventeen kidnapped girls have been freed from the clutches of the rioting marauders. Now it is your duty to see that they are married. We appeal to young people like you to come forward and take part in this virtuous act."

Perhaps somebody was giving a speech in that house.

Sushil, don't touch that broken glass with your bare fingers. Its sharp pointed edges will prick them, as they do my memories, bleeding them to a colour deeper than the deep red shard of glass.

References

1. Name of a Commercial Company
2. a Sikh
3. a part of a town
4. It is a double reed, conical, phonic (wind) instrument, made out of wood, with a metal flare bell at the end. It is common in North and West India and Pakistan during marriages, processions, and in temples.
5. It is a South Asian hand-drum widely used in devotional songs and various styles of film music.
6. The *doli,* also known as a palanquin, or *palkhi*, is a cot or frame, suspended by the four corners from a bamboo pole. Two or four men would carry it. In India, in the olden days, brides were carried in it to their groom's house.
7. Also called *mignonette tree*, is a flowering plant used since antiquity to dye skin, hair, fingernails, leather and wool. It is used in generally in India and Pakistan for dying the hands of brides fast red at the time of their marriage.
8. an Indian way of greeting with folded hands a person older than oneself
9. Hindi word for 'Mister'
10. a long piece of cloth worn by women in India, usually wrapped round the waist, tucked into a petticoat and given pleats with one end kept hanging over the shoulder.
11. the name of an Indian textile firm.
12. loose wide trousers with pleats below the knee, worn by women in North India.

7. THE BROKEN DOLL

Shakila Akhtar

The sight of his bride's stunning beauty stung his eyes like thorns. Niyaz felt the stinging pain tearing him apart. Her black eyes with long eyelashes made him extremely uneasy, a feeling he had not yet succeeded in fighting back. His concept of life was as unusual as it was bizarre. He loved darkness. Sad, long faces attracted him, and the pain oozing from soulful, frightened eyes, filled him with empathy. But oh, that cheerful, bright face, the quiver of those luscious lips! From where had they entered his life? He found his married life stifling, and tried his best to mask his quirky personality, though he didn't achieve much success in his effort.

Every nook and corner of his own house had suddenly changed out of his recognition. He discovered a new atmosphere surrounding the place, in which he found himself as a complete stranger. Oftentimes, he harked back wistfully to the days when he was the only occupant of his house, wallowing in his loneliness.

But little did he realize that even in those days he was never alone. There were the poor, and the oppressed, helping whom Niyaz always felt a strong sense of superiority. He was in love with his own self. He took delight in giving paisa coins to poor children playing in mud down the narrow lane of his decaying locality, feeling that his generosity would grant the dirty urchins some moments of smile. He performed that act of charity for sheer gratification of his self, and pleased at his graciousness, he would smoke heavily, sending curls in the air. He loathed light which exposed all the stitches of his wounded soul that were visible through the fine lines in his visage. Niyaz also hated the din and bustle surrounding high rising buildings. He passionately loved the sounds of dry, fallen leaves as they crunched under the shoes, producing some soft, plaintive, dying notes, followed by a prevailing silence.

Niyaz was very fond of his shabby neighbourhood. This was the place where he took refuge, after he had fled his home, dejected, broken-hearted. How could he bear the loss of someone with whom he had been intensely, innocently, in love since his childhood, playing with her in green fields, and running up and down the slops of lofty hay bales in barns? He fondly remembered her, holding whose delicate, small hands, his desires woke up as they grew from infancy to youth, and when he held out his hand to her to make her his own for ever, they were suddenly, quite mercilessly pushed away. He was still without a job. And no parent would give their daughter in marriage to a jobless man with an uncertain future.

Separated from the warmth of his home and the love of his mother, Niyaz left his past behind, his own identity, and walked out to a new place, a new house to start a new life. The fly ridden restaurant, roofed with tin and sackcloth, in front of his new abode, seemed to him to restore the warmth and affection that he had been missing. He had started feeling attachment even with the cracked and dirty cups and plates at the restaurant. All his broken relations appeared to him as restored, since the day he arrived at the place. He was the only white-collared, sophisticated visitor, occupying the wooden bench at the shoddy, inexpensive eatery, and was always greeted very respectfully by the waiters at the place, including the eatery owner. The darkness, the dinginess of the place, and the salutations of its occupants were now dearer to him than anything else.

He was well educated, and so after staying there for sometime, he got a good job and a suitable bungalow. But the change in his circumstances hardly brought any change in his lifestyle. After coming back from office he spent most of his time sitting, lost in thoughts, in a dark room of his new residence.

Though he loved his mother a lot, and had developed a passionate attachment to the dark corner of his house, his big ego sometimes compelled him to make great sacrifices. His unflinching narcissism led him to build a ring around his personality, and whenever anyone tried to break into that ring, Niyaz became furious, and felt like splitting from within. He would then gather with great difficulty all his scattered parts together and re-establish a fresh Narcissus, a Niyaz in all-consuming love with his own self. Bloated madly with self-love, Niyaz worshipped his self-made statue with an unshakable and abiding faithfulness. Every moment of his life danced perpetually around his own self, and that annular movement was, to him, no less sacred than walking round and round the Holy *Kaba*.

But there were moments when Niyaz dreaded his loneliness. The darkness of his house at times appeared to him as begging for light. The feeling that there was something missing in his life inexorably haunted him during those darker moments, though he was not still aware what his soul desired. He had everything that could keep one happy and satisfied, a comfortable house, a good job, loyal friends, nevertheless, he felt a loss of something that he couldn't himself say.

Sometimes, he struggled to discover his own self, his true identity, to understand himself, his desires. But every time, his love for the world, its people, and a yearning to rid them of suffering and pain, weighed heavy on his mind. Perhaps lurking behind that egocentric personality there was a strain of tender compassion, otherwise he would never have been so kind to the poor people in that dirty eatery. Their sad faces and the moist in their eyes melted him and pushed him to bring, though momentarily, some happiness in their lives.

As time went by Niyaz too, careless of everything around him, carried on feeding his insatiable ego, until suddenly, his friends and some of his distant relatives started pressing him strongly to get married. Hitherto, his arrogance had been successfully restraining him from falling under any outside influences. But at last his inflated egotism succumbed to mounting pressures from people he could not avoid. All escape routes had closed.

And when he caught the first glimpse of his wife on the wedding night, he was stunned. How radically different was that face from the one that often flashed through his mind's eye! He had always been avoiding the proximity of fragrant roses and vibrant flowers, to the extent that he was now quite incapable of admiring their delicate beauty. How then one who had never worn a flower in the buttonhole of his coat, could manage that vase of remarkable beauty, filled with fresh, delicate flowers? Niyaz pitied himself. They hadn't behaved well with him. His own friends had tried to rob him of his egoism. There was only one face, one picture, manifest in the dark recesses of his heart and mind, and that was his own. He had no room for another. Where would he fit that beautiful image sitting before him with all its embellishments?

Shahina's initiation into his life as his wife had thrown him into utter confusion. So far he was spending a happy and quiet life, after being dejected in love, a love that sapped before blossoming. Disgusted with the world, leaving his dear hometown and his mother's love behind, he had been breathing the fresh air of freedom for quite a few years, and now suddenly he felt as if heavy chains were fastened around his legs. Their jingles agitated him.

Step by step Shahina tried to enter into his existence, changing the darkness in his life to the brightness of morning. Her efforts started curtailing his self-acquired freedom. With her presence filling the house and his own life, he hardly found time to visit his favourite eatery as independently as before, until the children themselves showed up. Niyaz became uneasy on detecting the strains of displeasure in Shahina's eyes when she saw the shouting horde of dirty urchins at the bungalow. Unable to exercise the freedom of spending his money the way he liked, Niyaz felt he had his wings clipped. It was getting extremely difficult for him to go on tolerating the increasing assault on his independence, but he persevered for some time. And when he realized that Shahina's beauty was now running into his egoism, petrifying it, he at once rose to defend it, leaving aside all his good manners and modesty. His inner peace seemed suddenly shattered, and Niyaz became increasingly isolated from Shahina.

Shahina, who grew up in a household where she received immense love and affection, was heart broken when after marriage she found the glass palace of her dreams shattering into a thousand pieces. She was struck as if by lightning on discovering that she had stepped into a very different world. At first, her husband's bizarre behaviour jolted her a little, but she was quite sure that she would win Niyaz through her love and perseverance. Shahina tried hard to lighten the gloomy bungalow with her charming smiles, but Niyaz checked her advancing steps. Bright sparks of life kindled through her entire physical frame, but they gradually died out as she lost the strength to bear her husband's increasing and outspoken rudeness and rebukes. Patience, after all, has its own limits. Sometimes, she felt she would break into pieces if she tolerated him anymore.

Living through sighs and tears, Shahina bore a daughter to Niyaz within a year of her marriage. Niyaz loved children a lot no matter even if they were those dirty, stinking street urchins whom he met everyday. He longed to shower the same love and affection on his daughter, grew impatient to lock her in his passionate embrace, but somehow his open, outstretched arms shrank, and he drew back stunned. As he increasingly drew to her, hypnotized by her dazzling smile, her elfin, face, the pretty child, lying in the cradle with soft toys around her, displayed blithe indifference to him. He felt she didn't need his kindness, unlike Shahina. Shahina's daughter was just not the child who would be overjoyed to receive copper coins from Niyaz. In spite of being her father, he was still a stranger to her. Little by little, he started pulling away from the child. Shahina quietly watched the drama unfolding before her, but she could not bear for long the indifference that Niyaz was now displaying towards his daughter. She had till now tolerated all the taunts and jibes Niyaz had been throwing on her. But her husband's growing apathy first toward her and even more so towards the innocent child, convinced her that she could no more continue with a life fed on insults and hatred. At times she felt that all her inheritance of fortitude and fidelity lay trampled by the man's appalling ignorance and impulsive and aggressive behaviour.

Niyaz hated to see Shahina responding indifferently and carelessly to his nastiness. His bloated self-conceit expected her begging for his pity. But perhaps Shahina thought otherwise. And Niyaz hardly failed to notice the strong twitches of withering disdain in her eye muscles whenever he threw a nasty fit of temper. Very soon the exchanges of indignant looks gave way to bitter squabbles and verbal assaults.

Eventually, one day their quarrel took a very ugly turn. Niyaz, in one of his hysterical outbursts, abruptly asked Shahina to leave her house. She heard his dictate very patiently, and then phoned her parents, recounting, for the first time, the painful details of the story of her life. The next day, her parents arrived at the bungalow, and became furious when the saw their daughter's long, sad face. They decided, then and there, to put an end to her sufferings for ever, and take her out of the calamitous situation.

Niyaz, sitting in an adjacent room, was boiling with anger. He too wanted to get rid of her ominous presence which was threatening his freedom, and his narcissism, that he had been so fondly rearing. The mixed feeling of anger and relief at her wilful departure from his life welled up inside him. Shahina packed her belongings, and when she lifted her daughter from the cradle, her eyes suddenly turned to the picture on the wall, and settled there. *Why was her wedding picture with Niyaz still smiling after all that unhappiness and pain*? As she tried to remove the photo from the wall, the frame slipped from her trembling hands and fell on the bare ground, splintering into pieces. In her anxiety she stumbled on the fallen frame and the shards crunched beneath her naked foot fairly cutting it. Shahina looked down and saw that the colour of her blood had mixed inseparably with the colours in the picture. The spectacle of pain and pleasure was lying so obvious, so open, while inside her the strong contrasting colours of desire and despair, of the flaring of hope and the wreck of it, lay secretly and silently buried.

Niyaz sat unmoved in his room, hearing the rising and then falling noises in the house. He heard the car starting and then leaving his house, consigning him to his liberty and his ego. The house was turned into wilderness after a brief interval. There was silence everywhere. He walked over to Shahina's room, and stepped accidentally on the fragments scattered on the floor. They creaked and groaned under his shoes, but the picture lying on the floor was still smiling. His eyes glowed with happiness when he realized that the smile that had threatened to snatch his vanity, his self-love, has vanished. But when his eyes fell on the golden haired doll lying broken and lonely in the childless cradle, his heart strings suddenly started vibrating violently, and he became restless.

Tears coursed down his eyes, and picking the doll up, he clutched it to his chest, bringing it closer to his eyes, cuddling and kissing it passionately, crying in desperation, "My darling child! O, my little doll!"

All around the house, he found his own being, his existence, the self he loved madly, lying scattered in bits and pieces wherever his eyes could see.

8. THE PIGEONS OF THE DOME

Shaukat Hayat

A large flock of homeless pigeons was floating in the sky, in perfect symphony.

The hapless birds were flying unceasingly, now swooping low, circling over a specific area, perhaps looking desperately for their dwelling place, now flying away high in the sky, dejected and shocked at the sudden disappearance of the old dome, which had been there abode till it was pulled down to make way for new construction.

Their delicate wings must have become weary and exhausted from nonstop flight. He watched them as they swooped low just over his head, hovering slowly, looking with a baleful, haggard glare, their eyes inflaming as if all the blood had rushed there. It needed only to well up, and gush forth, and then they would pounce down in fury on whatever came within reach, flesh or fowl.

Thoughts veered through him, like the flight of birds, to the children who had now become a real nuisance for him, in the match-boxes like blocks of flats in his apartment building.

One needs to start rethinking fairly radically when human beings are compelled to live in hen coops, and hens are blessed with moving around freely in huge halls.

But children, after all, are children, whether they live in modern apartment blocks, or in huts and urban lanes and alleys. They are all equally unruly and wayward. Their noisy clamour would put the patience of sages to test. What was even more disquieting was that they, however, would suddenly get noisier and rowdier as they reached his flat to play with his children. He wondered whether that tiniest of flats in the largest apartment building in town, was the only place left for their mischief. In the name of carpet area, it had barely enough space for fewer people to breathe in and move their bodies. It was a windowless flat, quite like a hen house. The only place that gave him some relief was the small balcony, a large part of which was occupied by a number of pots filled with plants of brightly colored flowers—roses, jasmine, zinnia, crotons—the symbols of hope and life.

That day, exhausted after daylong work, he ascended the stairs, panting and puffing, to his fourth floor flat in the lift-less building, and as the door flung open, a bunch of children burst out, some clung to his feet; some climbed on his shoulders.

"Behave yourselves! What manners, eh . . . what manners? Be like good boys! Look, how quiet they are, as though they don't exist! That's why they are so singular!"

He craved for peace, as his mind wandered. *What more do you need in life, if you have enough time and tranquility to relax in an arm chair in your small balcony, a hot cup of tea in hand, and children staying busy and quiet! What greater pleasures await us in Heaven? What better remedy for weariness and fatigue?*

An enormous fig tree stood intact in the apartment campus, close to his flat, a few of its leafy branches stretching out into the balcony, partially shading it from the strong sun. The collage of solid cement structure standing with the evergreen fig tree presented a masterpiece of symbolic art.

He often sat in the balcony for hours after returning from work watching the same pair of sparrows hovering around, chirping brightly as if singing about the loveliness of life. Sometimes, a mischievous squirrel appeared on the balcony, stopped for a moment to gaze at him, and then scurried through the branch back to the fig tree. The sun's fainting light, filtering through the leaves, warmed somewhat the cool evening air, kindling his insatiable amorous passions. His mind buzzed with Bacchanalian delights, and he would hum softly to himself:

'O life, tone down thy cruelty!
Have gambled all I owned!
Yet know not if I've conquered thee,
Or even now you're far beyond!'

Brew bear with whisky, take a swig, its bitterness will make the brain reel! You'll suddenly become lighter, and feel like floating in the sky. Flying in stupor, look down on those walking on the earth. They'd appear no taller than pygmies.

Fierce wind usually swept through the place, shaking the leaves of the fig tree vigorously. Its little fruits would start falling steadily on the earth. In those moments, the chirping of sparrows mingled with the whistling of wind produced a strange aural sensation.

Sen Dada[1], his next-door neighbour, who always considered himself a young man at sixty-two, announced as he came out of his own flat, "It's good, the weather hasn't yet worsened as it did last year. I hope the day would pass peacefully. It's so pleasant and invigorating! Enjoy your life! There's nothing to worry at present."

He heard Sen Dada, as he was heading for the door, lost in anxious thoughts. *Why have the children chosen to throng into my flat? Are they holding any clandestine meeting? But why in my tiny flat, leaving their two and three-bedroom apartments? Everywhere the big fishes are devouring the small ones. Imagine what would happen if one day all the small fishes decide to attack the big fish together!*

The television in his flat was on, and the children were watching a quite modish programme on a private channel. He too was watching it quietly, thinking how enduring tradition and its values and decorum were sabotaged by the outrageous demands of modernity.

Before going out with Sen Dada, he muttered to his wife, "Can you tell the children how to behave? Ask them not to shout! These aren't good times. I'm afraid they're going to hurt my plants and even my flower pots! I've tended them with great care all these years. Please mind these rowdy boys! . . . Or listen! Wait a minute! Better leave it! Don't tell them anything. They're children after all, our neighbours' children. I'm sure they aren't going to cross their limits. Civilized people are, anyway, born to suffer!"

Dada tried to calm him down, "Don't worry, gentleman! Everything is going on normally. Bad situations don't usually last long. We can live peacefully only when we promote peace and stability. I, for one, can very clearly see that things are changing dramatically. The atmosphere around ensures happiness and harmony."

Sen Dada, an extremely orthodox kind of man, always spoke in a chaste, classical language whenever he was with him.

In the street below, traffic was flowing as usual. It was like any other weekend with a quite normal drop in the hustle and bustle of city life.

"My friend, what makes you look so mournful? I can understand you're worried the frolicking kids might destroy your plants and pots. But I assure you no such thing will happen. Your plants will be safe. We're going to meet our friends now, so stop looking gloomy! Enjoy your life! Look at that dome there; its round shape, its pointed prominence! It fills me with sheer ecstasy! Try looking at it yourself!" Sen Dada said, taking a long puff at his cigarette.

"Look at your age, Dada . . . !" He left the sentence deliberately unfinished.

Lost in the thought of a quite another dome, he was passing through a terrible mental state, while Sen Dada, on the other hand, was busy clucking at the sight of soft and fleshy corporeal domes.

"Why talk of ageing . . . feel young at heart, always . . . this is what life is all about . . . looking all around, watching intently life's colourful pageants, again and again . . . ! Young man, you're getting older in your youth . . . lift your eyes . . . look ahead!" Sen Dada continued his sermon tapping a little harder on his shoulder.

He suddenly saw three gorgeous damsels prattling along as they walked carelessly like doves, and realized the genesis behind Dada's impassioned reflections

"Forget your doves, Sen Dada! Look up, and watch those roving pigeons, hovering constantly in the sky above us! Rootless, unsafe birds! Their dwelling place has been quite savagely and stealthily demolished! How horribly are they suffering? Look into their eyes! You'll find blood welling up there, a desperate, burning desire to do something, washed by a feeling of helplessness."

But Sen Dada was overtaken by his own romantic obsessions. He didn't need to look up at the sky. The earth was very much with him, and on it there was no dearth of heavenly splendour. He was one of those elderly people whose eyes sparkled with concupiscence after their wives' death.

Leaving Sen Dada busy with his rambles, he recalled how everybody in the apartment building was terrified the other day, when the guard informed them that a huge, deadly snake was sighted in the parking area. Red alert was sounded in the entire building. Nobody slept that night. Clubs and sticks were collected from all over, and the windows and doors were closed. Terrified but alert, all eyes were on the watch. The fear of being bitten by the snake, if the eyes dropped to a doze or the light went out, lurked every moment.

But his big fear was that the snake might bite or scare away his pet squirrels and sparrows visiting the balcony everyday. The whole incident cast a dark cloud over the collage formed on normal days by merger of the colours of pots, flowers, squirrels and sparrows.

Taking a steel rod in his hand and a powerful torch, he had seated himself in the balcony where the sparrows had built a small nest. The melodious chirrups and coos of the small birds felt like the gurgling sound of coloured and bright water bursting forth from a fountain. He had guarded his balcony, for fear of the snake, for quite a few evenings and heaved a sigh of relief when nothing untoward happened. His wife, nevertheless, babbled away, reproaching him, asking him to get away from the balcony, scaring him from the snake's poison. But he had turned a deaf ear to her. Fed up with her intrusion, he told her at last to close the balcony door from inside, if she was so terrified, and leave him alone guarding the sparrows' nest. His wife and children entreated him, and finally left him alone, labeling him insane and stupid. But he was not ready, in any way, to leave the sparrows unsafe.

The apartment dwellers explored every nook and cranny of the building but the snake was not to be found. Every room, even the boxes and cupboards were searched without any success. The occasion awakened the children's natural curiosity, and they amused themselves by helping their elders with great alacrity, till tired and drawn, they slept wherever they were. The grown ups didn't sleep a wink the whole night, and when morning dawned they finally concluded that it was all a baseless rumour started to upset them. The finger of blame was pointed at the security guard of the apartment, who was accused of neglecting his duties.

Riding on the soft breeze of morning, silken butterflies came fluttering to the flowers on the balcony the following day. Bees swarmed around them. Small sparrows flew out of their nests to peck at grains on the ground. Soft and young rays of the sun embraced his balcony and he felt that life hadn't yet lost its meaning.

"Dada, I'm feeling quite uneasy! I don't know what might have happened to my flowers. Let's go back! I don't trust those unruly kids in my flat."

"You've lent yourself, to vain fancies! Every weekend the kids get together in a flat. It was your turn this weekend, and so they're there. And by the way, your children too are there with them. Come on . . . banish your worries now!"

"I'm beset by strange thoughts, Dada. The flying flock of homeless pigeons is sparking unknown fears in my mind. They are brutally deprived of their shelter. The lofty domes are licking dust now. Where will they go? Who's going to give them asylum . . . ?"

"Be positive, young man! There's a resting place everywhere around us, be they domes, towering peaks, stony caves, or massive trees in dense forests. Be ready to brave the vagaries of weather. You've to grow your skin a little tough to weather them, my friend!"

But deep inside, he could hear a mélange of different sounds, of cheers and fireworks shooting all around, alternated by a doleful tune played on a flute. The deafening sounds of pleasure and pain were spurting out simultaneously, freezing him to the spot, incapacitating him from thinking anything else. An atmosphere of confusion and absolute stillness prevailed around him, appearing to herald a fierce storm.

Insensitive to his overwhelming feelings of pain and pleasure, Sen Dada, on the other hand, was driven by his own lascivious appetite. He never missed to flash a coy look at the wives of friends they visited together. Paying courtesy calls to their friends, they arrived at Mr. Thompson's. A very cordial man, Mr. Thompson immediately took out a new bottle, and arranged glasses for them. Rica, his young housemaid, was helping him with the job.

She was moving quite nimbly, taking the lump of meat out of the fridge, slicing it into pieces, frying them, and then arranging them on a plate before the visitors. Hot steam rising from the fried steak sent a wave of tingling sensation down Sen Dada's body. Mr. Thompson shortly got dead drunk and quite lost. Sen Dada too was reaching that stage. He couldn't control himself when he saw Miss Rica offering a plate of semi-roasted cashew nuts to him, and placed his trembling fingers on her bare shin.

She lovingly took Dada's hands in hers, kissed them with respect, and preparing a peg for him, lifted the glass to his lips. Dada's life long thirst was quenched and he was composed for a moment. But the very next moment a great restlessness seized upon him, and he felt blood racing through his veins. His fingers once again started crawling through Rica's naked shin up to her shapely thighs.

Rica was taken aback at Dada's sudden amorous advances. Her face, though, was devoid of any expression. She did not put up any resistance, and Dada's fingers crawled up faster.

Suddenly tears welled up in Rica's eyes.

She looked blankly at Sen Dada, and was lost in the valleys of the past, recalling her childhood, listening to the distant voices,

"My loving daughter, Rica . . . !"

"Life is an endless sky . . ."

"You've to go a long way . . . a very long way . . ."

Her affectionate father had cherished many pleasant dreams for Rica. She remembered she always clung to her father's arm, and climbed on his shoulder, when he uttered those loving words to her. Mr. Sen's resemblance with her father had instantly drawn her towards him. Her father now lay entombed in a coffin.

After his death, Rica drifted helplessly like leaves flying on the wings of winds. Wandering from place to place, she finally reached Mr. Thompson's safe haven. He was looked up with great respect in the vicinity. Here, she had to feign laughter and happiness under enormous pressure, and surrender herself to the man.

Rica had no other options, after having knocked many doors and being greeted at each of them by slobbering beasts, sticking out their tongues, staring at her with blood in their eyes. Mr. Thompson wasn't as bad as them. He was a well perfumed, neat and clean man. His touch never aroused any feeling of repulsion in her, nor offended her aesthetic sensibility. Entirely unaware of Rica's mental state, Sen Dada was absorbed in his own world of inebriation and lewdness. The rush of overwhelming feelings fluttered his eyes shut, while she stood beside him, though quite unwillingly.

Even in his drunken state, Mr. Thompson saw through Dada's lewd intentions. He was a generous man, and although he did welcome others' share wholeheartedly in his cakes and ales, he was not at all ready for any partnership in his personal possession.

He cast a furious look at Rica, and the poor girl, whose eyes had brimmed with sympathy for Dada, was confounded to find Mr. Thompson staring at her. She quickly collected the empty plates and marched towards the kitchen. She stayed there till Mr. Thompson called her out for some work.

All that while, he was sitting quietly, watching Dada, Thompson, and Rica, and wondering whose pain was greater, Rica's or his own. He felt, then, as if the flock of cooing pigeons were hovering over his head, and got his answer there. Surely, the suffering of the homeless pigeons was far greater than theirs! The unfortunate birds had to endure the torment of exile for their entire life. They had been denizens of the dome for many generations. But now . . .

He was filled with anger at the drinking spree of the two older people. Sen Dada always delivered his sermon, "Young man, forget pains . . . enjoy life!"

How could one enjoy when everything seemed to fall apart?

Suddenly, the sound of falling dishes and utensils from the inner quarters of the house filled the room.

Rica burst into the room terrified, "Uncle . . . a pigeon has fluttered into our house! The cat at the next-door house was going to prowl on it, when the poor bird strayed into our kitchen, and hid behind the small pile of plates and bowls. I've driven the cat off with difficulty, and closed the door of the kitchen."

A strange fear gripped him as he heard Rica, and he peeped into the eyes of Dada and Mr. Thompson. They too appeared totally mystified at the news, in spite of being heavily drunk. Their heads drooped as if a catastrophe had struck them. There was a knock at the main door at that very moment.

"Mr. Thompson . . . Mr. Thompson . . . !"

Sad and scared, Rica opened the door. The neighbour from the adjacent house was standing at the door, "Miss Rica . . . call Mr. Thompson, please . . . !"

"What happened man?" Mr. Thompson completely drunk, wobbled towards the door, with heavy, unsteady steps.

"My pigeon has entered your house . . . you know my mother-in-law is an old patient . . . these days her hands are often numb from elbows down. The doctor has advised her to take pigeon soup. I was trying to slay it when it escaped and flew into your house."

"Yeah man, yea . . . that bird . . . scared . . . hid at my place . . . Rica found it . . . that blasted cat . . . its enemy . . . Rica . . . give 'im 'is bird! Come, you, Mr. John! 'ave some drink!"

"Oh no, thanks! I drink on Saturdays only. I don't have to get up early on Sundays. I feel extremely sleepy after boozing up a lot!"

Distressed and hesitant, Rica finally brought the pigeon back from the kitchen. She was badly trembling and muttering to herself. Mr. Thompson watched her mumbling to herself but could not make any sense of what she was saying.

Her eyes were expressionless while her lips were moving, "*Wretched little thing . . . fly away if you can't fight . . . hurry . . . flee . . . far . . . far from human habitation . . . make off to the huge sky or to the forests . . . quick!*"

But the scared bird cowered in her hands, perhaps with some apprehension. And as Mr. John, thanking her, stretched his hands out to catch hold of the pigeon, Rica felt something suddenly leapt out from her inside.

He rested on the sofa, quietly observing the entire episode unable to decide who was more timorous; Rica or the horrified pigeon. Or was he himself trembling in fear, much more than them?

A thought suddenly crossed his mind, *What if the unfortunate bird knew it was going to be slaughtered? Perhaps one from the flock might have been slain earlier to tender warmth and movement to the old woman's stiff hands . . . !*

Rica inadvertently loosened her grip on the bird. A strange force from within her leapt out and jerked her hands violently. *Fly away if you can't fight! Oh you little creature, have you lost the strength?*

Freed from her grasp, the pigeon flew away and perched on the skylight.

Mr. Thompson slapped hard on her face. He was enraged. Miss Rica was thunderstruck. Thompson ordered her to put up a high stool on the table and catch the bird. She tried to mount on it to reach to the skylight, but slipped, and fell hard on the floor. Perhaps, she was badly hurt. Sen Dada got up to lift her, but Mr. Thompson reached her first, and hauled her up to her feet, clutching her to his chest. She was badly trembling.

No one seemed to be aware of his presence, not an eye fluttered in his direction, as he witnessed the drama unfolding before him, the threesome Mr. Thompson, Sen Dada, and the poor girl, each venting their own strong emotions.

Sen Dada, dejected at his botched romantic overtures, came back to the sofa, held his hand, and pulling him up, took leave of Mr. Thompson, saying, "We'd like to leave now, Mr. Thompson! Thanks a lot! We really enjoyed your company!"

"But this gentleman, your friend, looks so grief-stricken! I don't think he was pleased to be here!"

Sen Dada patted softly on his shoulder with great affection, though his sly looks were constantly chasing the still trembling Rica.

"His sorrow may be justified if it's going to alleviate his agony. But I know it's not. I brought him here thinking a pint or two would soothe away his worries. On the contrary, the cat and bird game has made him even sadder. Don't worry. Everyone brings his own luck. You've shown great generosity of spirit. Thank you very much for your warmth!"

Dada took a close look at Rica before leaving the place. She was looking dazzlingly beautiful even in her fright.

"Bye . . . bye Rica! Bye Mr. Thompson! Good night!"

They visited a few more friends that day. Everybody they met tried to shirk away from talking about the snake rumour. People in the apartment building were privately, either happy or sad, but all desisted to express their feelings. They were all affected by the incident in their own ways. But they all felt equally helpless, and despite their apparent nonchalance, one question haunted them all.

What will happen now? How are we going to react if anything untoward happens?

He had now got bored moving along with Sen Dada. He too had drunk, but far from getting inebriated, he did not even feel drowsy. The picture of the plants, the balcony, and the band of boys there kept moving before his mind's eye. A strange suspicion overpowered him while he was making the rounds with Sen Dada.

After enjoying his visits to his friends at the building, Sen Dada finally decided to return. He was staggering. Intoxication had subsumed his entire being. The brief sensual intimacy with Rica had invigorated his intoxication, but even then he could not forget to console his fellow-walker. He comforted him about the well-being of his flowers, plants, and pots.

Throughout their way back, Sen Dada cheered him up as though he was caressing and fondling a child, saying, '*Don't you worry, child! Everything will be Okay*!'

The guard at the apartment building waved them as they moved out. There was silence all around. Had he not helped Sen Dada climb the stairs to his flat, he would have certainly stumbled. Reaching the third floor to Dada's flat, he had to hold him and take the key to his flat from out of his pocket, with great difficulty. He opened the door and after settling him inside his flat safely, and getting assured that Dada had locked the door from inside, he came out and proceeded to his flat. His legs trembled as he was taking the stairs to his flat. A mysterious fear was fuelling within him.

His wife answered the call bell, and he could clearly see that her eyes were swollen as when one cries hard and long.

"How are my flowers and . . . ?"

"Go . . . see yourself!" She spoke with great difficulty.

The children were in deep sleep in their beds. Their faces were frozen, contorted in agony. Perhaps they were watching a horrible and painful dream. And his fears finally proved well-founded when he stepped into the balcony. The appalling spectacle suddenly seized him, virtually paralyzing him with fear and pain. Flowers lay scattered, plucked out of their pots, their petals crushed and squeezed on the mosaic floor; the earth from the pots littered hither and thither; the twigs that once constituted the birds' nest lay broken; the sparrows were nowhere to be seen; squirrels, butterflies, and bees had disappeared perhaps never to return in near future. The life and beauty of his balcony had gone to the dust.

So, finally the children in their amusement and fun-making had ruined everything.

His guess was correct. That day, the snake had sneaked into their apartment offering the children a diversion as gory as it could be. They had played the dangerous game of death and destruction with the snake, and its deadly end-result was before his eyes. Smothered, floral fragrance lay stifled; innocence played with fire causing its own destruction.

The bloody-eyed flock of pigeons was still flying high in the sky, looking for some shelter, perhaps working into a frenzy, a passion, to accomplish something however unseemly.

He returned to his room, and when his eyes met his wife's, he realized that there was a dead body lying in the flat and its burial was a big problem as there was curfew outside.

9. THE MAGICAL PARROT

Pervez Shahidi

My living room is a usual meeting place, a kind of pilgrimage for my friends. They visit it as religiously as palmers their Holy Land. My house has become their favourite haunt, though my pecuniary concerns can seldom endure everyday expenses of cigarettes, *paan*[1] and tea. But the trouble is that, living all by myself, I too cannot afford to abandon their company and spend my time in isolation. Whenever they are free from work, they while away their time at my place, offering me occasion to thank them for their interesting company. I avoid calling on them for reasons listed below, and they have willingly agreed to settle on my house as our weekend meeting place exactly for the same reason.

Shakir lives with his wife and children, and his house only bedrooms. Someone or the other is always sick at Mahmoud's house. There is only one sitting room at Amjad's which the women folks in and around his house often fill in, and a family of diehard religious conformists that they are, there is no place for us there. Yousef lives in a one-room flat with his younger brothers. Razi lives where the town ends, and we can hardly afford to travel that far as frequently as we wish. My house, on the other hand, has only two occupants, my servant and my own self. Besides, I live at a centrally located place which falls on the way to most offices where my friends work. With no family to tend to, I can enjoy the privilege of friends, coming to me for expending their time and guttural energy to the best of their choices, which is just not possible in their respective houses.

Didn't someone say that it is one of the blessings of old friends that you can afford to be stupid with them? And after all the curse of cunning and craft plaguing the world, isn't it wiser to play the fool sometimes with friends who make your uninteresting house suddenly buzz with activity, making it look like a classy bungalow of some importance?

Neighbours usually ask me, "Why visitors keep on flocking to your house? What's so attractive there?"

I tell them quite self-confidently, "O, I've much to allure them. We've cards, chess, *chausar-pachisi*[2], carom etc. to play, and when we get bushed, we indulge in inconclusive arguments and animated discussions. Everyone has to shed some light on such diverse and interesting topics as poetry, literature, philosophy, psychology, politics etc. Occasionally, we have poetry recitals too."

But these days our talks revolve around international relations, the future of the world, events in Germany, Russia, Britain, Turkey, Finland etc., and the Congress and the Muslim League back home. Of all these, the issue that beckons our attraction the most relates to women and their role in society. We discuss this particularly freely and exhaustively, recounting our own individual experiences and stories. Very few of us, perhaps, are blessed in this mad, hurly-burly world of ours with the pleasure of such a rollicking company.

This blessing comes not by the sweat of brow
Till caring God does not His Grace bestow!

It was only yesterday that all my bosom buddies gathered at my humble dwelling sharp at six in the evening, except Razi and Yousef as usual. Each of us was eloquently displaying our own awareness of poetry. We discussed *Ghalib*[3], and Amjad recited one of his famous verses, tunefully,

Oft kills my mirth my restless heart, and warns me that,
The shade of yonder leafy bough's a snake in fact?

Everyone swayed passionately from side to side. We were still in raptures when Shakir suddenly spoke out, "Friends! Though I don't get frenzied like Ghalib, yet I have always had a similar hallucination in the garden during dark nights. It's not at all strange to mistake the shady boughs as snakes. In fact, a few times I have seen ghosts and witches sitting on trees during nights. It's quite difficult to tell you how those macabre appearances had petrified me!"

The assemblage fell into a long conversation on ghosts, and poor Ghalib and his poetry receded from their mind. Everyone was raring to recount his encounters, actual or fictional, with the spirits. We were so mesmerized by Shakir's crazy, tall, and fragmented stories that we never realized when and how the real topic of conversation got changed. Amjad too jumped on the ghost story bandwagon with his own ghostly experiences. Every story teller was cutting the other off in his enthusiasm, until he himself was prevented from completing his own account.

The stories had not yet reached their climax when we heard a loud knock. I dashed to the door to find Rafiq, my long-time friend, standing there. This particular gentleman had returned to India only two months ago, after a gap of six years, on completing his doctorate in philosophy from Cambridge. It was my second meeting with him after his return from England.

I very cordially welcomed him, "Hello, Rafiq! Come in my friend! Long time, no see! So good of you to remember your old buddy!"

"I'm so sorry, my friend! I was really busy all these days, trying hard to find a teaching job at a university here. Believe me, had I have free time I'd have visited you that instant."

I introduced Rafiq to the assembled company. After customary hellos and warm handshakes we took our seats. I looked at the empty cigarette cases and called my servant out, "Sub . . . ha . . . a . . . n! Would you please bring us a few packs of *Cavenders*, and some *paans*? And please get them fast! Remember, you've to prepare tea, too!"

Worried at not getting any reply, I went to him, and taking him aside, whispered, "Why . . . what's the matter? Why don't you go?"

"Sir, the *paan* and cigarette sellers have now stopped lending on credit! They say they want their arrears first." The servant reached the message to my ears with profound sadness and politeness.

"You silly fellow! Is this the time to explain all that to me? Go assure him all his dues will be paid tomorrow! Win him over, anyhow, to loan you the things. Can't you see the guests are waiting! Do you want to embarrass me before them?"

Subhan, accustomed to the awkward but usual situation, said nothing and went out.

I returned to my chair and turned towards Rafiq, "We were talking about something very interesting before you entered. Why don't you throw some light on it? You're a philosopher. You can come up with your interesting analysis"

"What's that? Tell me, please, what has been engaging you all!" Rafiq blurted with a sense of pride.

"We're talking about metaphysical realities, on the existence of genies, ghosts, witches, etc. Everyone present here has had some kind of experiences with these supernatural elements. We hope you'll enlighten us with your understanding." Amjad responded with extreme seriousness.

"Oh no gentlemen, I'm too small to have any big thought on the topic! Anyway, I can tell you about my personal experiences, but not before enjoying some of yours." Rafiq said, with his customary humility.

"Well Amjad, why don't you start your story from the beginning? Rafiq too would perhaps like to hear it." I requested him restlessly.

Amjad's story was yet incomplete, and our aural curiosity still insatiable. The servant had brought *paans* and cigarettes in the meantime.

"Mr. Amjad, I'm also waiting for you story. Please retell your experience!" Rafiq echoed me, lighting his cigarette.

Pulling on his cigarette, Amjad started recounting his harrowing experiences with extraordinary seriousness. He narrated numerous small incidents—his bumping into a big black cat on a dark Friday night street; his throwing stone on the black devil, inviting blazing flames bursting from the creature's eyes; his returning home that night and seeing horrible visions and dreadful faces in his dreams; the catastrophic consequences of poisonous evil tongues; and waking up in deep sleep on some nights, on hearing shrill, disembodied voices. Everyone listened to him in rapt silence till Amjad took a deep long breath and finished his weird snippets.

Tea was laid down on the table, and I announced frankly, "Gentlemen, please enjoy your tea without any formalities!"

"Don't worry! We'll take care of ourselves." Shakir came forward with his rare openness.

"Well, I think it's your turn now Rafiq! We'd like you to tell us some of your encounters? We are more than eager to hear them." I tried to draw their attention to the burning topic of that evening.

"Let me first finish my tea! What's the hurry?" Rafiq returned laughingly.

"Alright then, I'm going to relate my dull and bland experiences, till Mr. Rafiq finishes his tea." Shakir asked our permission very humbly.

"O, sure! You needn't be so modest! We'll enjoy even if they are dull." Rafiq encouraged him.

Heartened by our support, Shakir narrated his tale,

"One night when it was utterly dark all around, I walked out of my house. It was a humid, summer night, and the electric supply had suddenly snapped. I was strolling in the front garden when my eyes fell on a huge fig tree standing there. I saw a weird looking black woman sitting on a bough with her legs dangling. I was suddenly horrified to notice that her feet were inverted, heels and toes, back to front. Terrified, I ran back towards my house. A strange and frightening nasal voice followed me down, and I fainted on reaching my room. My wife and children woke up at the noise, and brought me somehow to my senses. For full two days after that incident, I was laid up with high fever and spasms of tremor in the body."

Though we enjoyed Shakir's bizarre story, we all felt a shade of fear lurking inside us. I then asked Mahmoud to come up with his experiences, but he excused himself, and pointing towards Rafiq, spoke out, "Wouldn't it be better if Mr. Rafiq agrees to narrate his brush with the spirits. My experiences are very similar with Shakir's. I don't have any new thing to say."

"It's fine, then! Please come out with your story, Rafiq? We're anxiously waiting!" I placed my request before him.

"Alright, but on one condition only!"

"What's that?" I was surprised.

"It's very simple. I must be allowed to complete my tale without any interruption. A small break and the story will become insipid." Rafiq laid down his condition very categorically.

"Come on! We aren't so uncivilized. Take it easy, and start!" I reassured him.

"But my story raises five intriguing questions, of which I shall tell you later. Listen then, and ponder at the shortcomings and imperfections of science and philosophy." Rafiq grasped the situation quickly and readied himself to begin.

We lit our cigarettes, and Rafiq started his strange account,

"Once, I traveled to London, on my annual vacation from Cambridge University. I checked into a cheap hotel, because I intended to spend my entire long vacation there. A few days later, to amuse myself, I walked out in the evening, strolling leisurely down Wellford Street. Incidentally, my eyes landed on a wooden plate hanging on the door of an old looking house, with the word '*Haunted*' inscribed on it. An extremely inquisitive person that I am, I got the owner's address from a nearby shop, and headed towards his residence.

Mr. Gibson, the owner of the awe-inspiring house, lived a mere fifty-sixty yards away from the place, with his wife and little daughter, in a rented flat. On reaching there, I sent my visiting card and was immediately ushered in. He welcomed me warmly and asked me the purpose of my visit. I talked about the haunted house I had seen on my way, and expressed my wish to take it on rent.

Mr. Gibson looked surprised at my courage. He gave an account of some very horrible incidents regarding the house, and tried to dissuade me from renting it. But my interest by now had turned into an insatiable curiosity, and inundated with my repeated requests, he finally handed over the keys on my own responsibility. The three pound monthly rent was too good an offer to reject. Perhaps, he had reduced the rent to the pettiest amount considering the fact that no one would knowingly like to occupy a ghost ridden house.

I took the keys, thanked him, came back to the hotel, checked out from there, got into a taxi with my luggage, and landed at the house. Unlocking the front door, I entered the house, and looked carefully into every room. Each of the rooms was arranged with chairs and tables of different shapes and styles. The bedroom was quite comfortable. After preparing my bed, arranging my books on the table, and my clothes in the wardrobe, I headed to the washroom, freshened myself, changed my clothes, and walked out of the house to the nearest restaurant. It was around eight o'clock in the evening when I returned to my new abode, picked up Sir Oliver Lodge's '*Why I Believe in Personal Immortality*' from the table, got into my bed, and started reading it with great interest.

A distant tower clock struck twelve, and I was startled to realize it was time to sleep. Putting the book aside, as I was preparing to sleep, my eyes wandered on the strange shapes forming on the wall in front. I hadn't, at first, cared to look at the wall. There was a picture frame hanging just in the middle of the wall with a parrot's picture in it. I looked up intently at the picture. And lo . . . what was that? The parrot suddenly started shaking. Its beak was moving up and down. Though the bizarre sight utterly stunned me with horror, I gathered enough strength, picked up my shoe, and aimed it at the picture. The shoe was still in my hand, when to my growing dread I saw the mysterious parrot changing its form.

In a magical moment, the parrot changed into a very beautiful young woman. More than just a picture, it looked like an angelic form sticking to the wall, standing right in front. Her symmetrical shape, thin lips, glassy, slanting eyes, flushed, chubby cheeks, and long black hair reaching below her waist, captivated me completely. Her fixed, vacant stare rendered me absolutely motionless. It was like an ocean of beauty flooding my entire being, and all my senses. My heart and mind were carried away on its gigantic tidal waves. My eyes were frozen on the figure. I cannot say how long I remained fixed in that state. On regaining my senses, I got up, and rushed hysterically to grasp the form. But to my astonishment, it evaporated in a flash, leaving the frame, with the picture of the still parrot returning in its place.

I touched the picture, groped around it, and started at it for some time. It didn't change, nor did it move. The picture wasn't now displaying anything unusual. Picture frames are the embellishments of the walls. They adorn them to give us pleasure and thrill. But the picture of the magical parrot evoked a strange sweet pain down my heart. My eyes started searching the captivating form, in vain. Seized by a great and painful restlessness, I kept looking impatiently, groping at the wall for the soulless figure. My mind whirled through raving imaginings of the vanished form for a long while.

My senses came back to me when the morning rays of the sun, filtering in through the windows, shone on my face.

Their warmth stirred me into action. I freshened myself up, and went out for breakfast. On my way to the restaurant, my mind wandered to the image of last night's bewitching beauty, the visionary gleam that had lighted up my amorous desires. Her beauty was enchanting enough to test the patience of yogis.

An overwhelming passion, welling up inside me, reassured me, nevertheless, that I was going to see her again. I had a quick breakfast at the restaurant, and wandered through the nearby streets and lanes the whole day, till the street lamps twinkled in the gathering dust. Deciding to end my daylong roving, I took my evening meal, and reached my residence at about nine at night.

Fatigue and hopelessness didn't allow me to indulge in librocubicularism, and, therefore, I half-stretched on my bed, fixing my eye on the parrot at the front wall, waiting impatiently for the celestial beauty to manifest her. My heartbeats raced as the wait grew longer. I felt frail and frozen every hopeless moment. Every minute, my despair seemed to mock at me.

The anxious wait finally ended after about three hours, as I detected the parrot making motions. The movement of the beak and wings continued for some time, and then the magical bird was transformed into the previous night's stunning beauty, standing enchantingly before me. Her attractive, delicate features appeared more entrancing than the last night. Her ruby lips quivered for the first time. Her silvery arms stretched out as if inviting me for an embrace. Her beauty shook me out of my dazed stupor. I dashed to the wall and held my hands against it, trying to clutch the arms. Time flew away, taking the object of my desire with it. I recovered my normal self after some time, and realized that the wall had nothing on it except the lifeless picture of the parrot pasted in a frame.

The day had broken, and my stupor too broke with it. The appearance and disappearance of the beguiling form continued with the dance of my days and nights. My nights were spent in fits of passion, my days in roaming aimlessly through the streets, highways, restaurants, dance houses, cinema halls, and theatres. Men, old women, and young girls, filling those places, never received even my cursory glances. My eyes were continuously searching the face that had now become my consuming passion. But the face to which I had mortgaged my time and eyes was not yet to be seen on the streets of London.

One full month passed in my desperate search and restless wanderings. Nights of passion and fulfillment continued with the days of loss and longing. I wished all my days turned to those mesmerizing nights, but wishes refused to be horses. I was getting despondent to the brink of thinking of ending my own life.

And one day, when I was on my usual diurnal wanderings, my eyes fell on a roadside hoarding displaying a Spanish circus which was going to start its show from that very day. I decided to amuse my sagging spirit, and headed towards the circus. Evening was closing, and the show was to start in a few minutes. I bought a ticket for the third class and entered the big top. The show started almost half hour after I entered.

Acrobatics, unicyclists, trapeze acts, jugglers, horse rides, animal shows with elephants and lions, succeeded one after the other entertaining my sad mood. And then my eyes caught sight of a few beautiful girls in red dresses, entering the ring, dancing in a circle. The movements of their hands and feet were displaying the mastery of performing art. A sea of melody and music was swelling all around. For some time they all danced separately, and then in circles. When their rotary motion came to a halt, a veiled figure dressed in black, riding a horse, singing a Spanish song in doleful tune, suddenly entered the ring and came near the circle of dancing girls.

Cheering shouts of "*Isabella*", "*hey . . . hey, Miss Isabella*", went up from the fervent crowd of spectators sitting in the tiered seating. I asked the gentleman sitting beside me the reason for such a passionate show of enthusiasm.

Annoyed at my ignorance, the man retorted, "Haven't you read this morning's newspaper? Every daily worth its name has published columns on Isabella's exquisite beauty. Look she's removing her veil now!"

The moment her delicate, sparkling feature was exposed to my naked eyes, I was shocked to see that it was the same woman who appeared every night from the picture frame at the '*Haunted*' house. I got up from my seat, and rushed blindly towards her, shouting, "*There she's . . . O heavens . . . that's really her*!"

As a corollary to my passionate impetuosity, my legs tackled the chairs that missed my eyes, and I toppled over them, falling unconscious. When I regained my consciousness I found myself lying in a hospital bed.

The doctor forbade me as I tried to get up, “Keep lying, please! You’re still under deep shock!”

“I’m feeling quite fine, doctor! Please, let me go home! I’ll die if I stay here any longer.” I pleaded desperately.

“I’m sorry, sir! I’m bound by law to not allow you to leave in your present mental state.” The doctor’s tone was harsh.

He gestured to the nurse, and she administered some medication to me after which I slept soundly the whole night. The next morning, after repeated pleadings and assurances, I was allowed to leave the hospital. I had my tea and breakfast at a restaurant in the vicinity, and then took a taxi straight to the circus. The entrance to the large and gaudy circus tent was closed, so I made several rounds of it, trying to peep into it from some tiny holes in the tent. I also asked about Miss Isabella from the circus workers moving around. Considering me a moonstruck lover, they laughed, and jeered at me, and walked away. Embarrassed at their strange behaviour, I couldn’t but endure what befell me. Hopeless and distraught, I reached my ‘*Haunted*’ house.

As evening dawned, I put on my expensive evening suit, thrust two five pound bills into my trouser pocket, and reached the circus. I bought a first class ticket, entered the arena, and sat in the first row, very close to the ring. The show started, as usual, on time, and after many electrifying performances, the dancing girls appeared again, in a circle. They suddenly stopped dancing, when the curtain was raised, and veiled Isabella entered the ring, riding a lion. Reaching the centre of the ring, with the girls around her, she pulled her veil back, and dismounted from the lion. With excitement bubbling up inside me, I felt like jumping out of my chair, rushing towards her. But I quickly controlled my wild ravings, anyhow, and started watching her very intently. She was dancing elegantly in slow motion, and surrounding her, the girls too were moving musically and gracefully in a circle.

Isabella had started singing a melodious Spanish folk song. I hadn't heard a sweeter, more velvety voice. My heart too danced with the ebb and flow of her voice. The mesmerizing performance of her body and voice was of a level where thoughts could seldom reach. The fairness of her skin contrasted strikingly with her black dress, stunning my senses. She walked out of the circle, dancing with the same elegance, synchronizing her movements with the flow of music, and came to the edge of the ring. Our eyes suddenly met and locked together perhaps in a battle of wills. She stood smiling for a moment, and then turned back to accompany her troupe, vanishing behind the curtain.

I was lost in her charm, soaked in hopes and delight, when my eyes caught hers, peering from behind the curtain, acknowledging the deafening and enthusiastic applauses from the audience. The curtain was drawn and the show ended, leaving me in rapturous painfulness. I came out of the tent, headed to a nearby restaurant, gulped my food, and hurried back to the circus ready to watch the last show of the day.

The same human and animal shows repeated themselves, failing by all means to kindle my enthusiasm and interest in the banal performances, but succeeding in kindling my hopes of meeting Isabella every other moment. After a rather long wait, the curtain was raised, and some girls, dressed and dancing like fairies, entered the ring. They had delicate wings spreading out from their sides, and they were holding a throne on their shoulders. As they appeared on the stage, I could clearly see Isabella sitting on the throne, looking like a fairy queen.

The throne was placed on the ground, and the girls started swirling round and round it. The fairy queen was gracing the throne in all her majesty and charm. She held a small golden hand fan in her soft, silky hand, and was waving it slowly with a great poise. Every movement of the fan was fanning my latent passionate intensity. The girls stopped the dance and kissed the legs of the throne, and the beauty queen responded with a charming smile. Taking their hands in hers, she descended from the throne in a marvelous choreography of movement, singing a rapturous Spanish song fused with fascinating music. My heart and mind leapt out of my physical existence and wandered to strange lands of delightful sounds and luscious beauty.

The song ended, and Isabella ascended her throne. The girls again lifted the throne and smiling back at me she left the stage with them, disappearing behind the curtain. I took my hat and went out, after waking from my stupor. Shuttling between hopes and despair, I reached my residence, got into my night dress, and reclining in my bed, started my nocturnal passion, gazing at the hide and seek game between the parrot and the peerless beauty.

I continued spending my evenings at the circus, locking my eyes with the dazzling eyes of Isabella, relishing her presence and her youthful splendour, while my nights were spent gazing at the parrot of the '*Haunted*' house, watching with amorous delight, the emergence of Isabella from out of the bird's figure. The more I saw her, at the circus and at my lodging, the more my passion for her grew stronger and uncontrollable. I now longed to meet her and talk to her. My heart was restless to express my feelings and emotions. Compelled by the force of passion, one day I went to the manager of the circus, and placed my request before him.

But the heartless man shattered all my hopes, "I'm sorry, gentleman! No stranger is allowed to meet her."

I only wished I were rich enough to buy his permission to have a rendezvous with her. Finding it impossible to chase my wishes, I contented myself with gazing unblinkingly at her during my tryst with her at the circus and my residence. More than a fortnight passed with little change in my inflexible routine.

One day, I couldn't go to the circus because of a severe pain in my stomach. I lay in bed the whole evening, talking to the parrot, waiting for it to disappear, and it did so when the clock struck twelve. But to my surprise the captivating beauty didn't emerge from the empty frame. Shooting stomach pain conspired with the heartbreak, making me restive and distraught. I spent the entire night scuttling between the bed and the front wall. When the light of the early morning sun stole in through the windows, I found, to my utter dismay, that along with the phantom of my delight, the picture of the parrot had also disappeared from the wall. The parrot, my only hope of that passionate vision, was also lost now, and I lay in bed flustered and flummoxed.

After some while, my transitory infatuation was overtaken by a stronger feeling of hunger. I got out of bed, and after a shower and change of dress, headed towards the restaurant. A daily visitor to the place, I had become quite friendly with the restaurant manager.

He came to my table while I was sipping tea, and said, "Good morning, sir! Yesterday, you weren't at the circus, perhaps? A terrible disaster struck there last evening! Haven't you read the morning newspaper?"

"Oh no, I had a bad pain in my stomach, I couldn't go there yesterday. Is everything fine? I really don't know what happened there." I asked him, visibly perturbed.

"Oh, really! Don't you know that last night the lion at the circus fatally wounded Miss Isabella? She was immediately taken to the hospital, but the poor woman died on way." The manager informed me sadly.

I got up with a jerk, and asked him frantically, "Is that really true? Miss Isabella . . . the circus girl . . . the same Miss Isabella . . . she's dead . . . not in this world now . . . tell me please . . . answer me!"

"I'm not kidding, sir! I gain nothing by lying to you. Look at this newspaper! See here! Read it yourself! It's nine o'clock now. The funeral must be arriving. They're taking it down this way to the graveyard." He informed me, and went away.

I picked up the newspaper. It carried the tragic news on the front page, in bold black letters. I froze. A flood of raging passion welled up inside me, and tried to inundate my entire existence. I called the waiter and ordered for some wine. I drank heavily and smoked like a chimney to keep my torment under control. But the more I did so the more I grew jittery and hideously inebriated.

The manager rushed to me, on being informed by the hotel boy, and whispered in my ear, "Are you okay, sir? Shall I call a taxi to get you home?"

"Thank you so much, Mr . . . . ! You're a very nice man! Please do me a favour! Take me with her funeral procession to the graveyard! I'm fainting . . . I can't go alone . . . help me, please!"

Her hearse arrived soon. The manager called a taxi, and got in somehow with me and followed the funeral cortege. After her burial, the man took me to his restaurant. I hadn't yet regained complete consciousness, so he deposited me in a Victoria chair, where I fell into deep sleep.

When I got up, it was already six in the evening. Thanking the kind manager, I walked to my residence. The parrot had disappeared along with the picture frame. The wall stood blank and hopeless. I felt horror and loneliness all around. It appeared as if the walls too were in mourning. It was now unbearable for me to stay there any longer. So, I packed my luggage, called a taxi, and moved to the hotel where I was staying before renting the '*Haunted*' house. I started spending my days and nights drinking like a fish. The hotel keeper tried to assuage my sufferings, but soon lost all hope when he realized that there wasn't a snowball's chance in hell that I would change.

Incidentally, Mr. Iqbal, one of my Cambridge pals, arrived one day at the hotel, perhaps for a short stay. On learning form the manager about my presence there, he bumped into my room one morning. I was busy drinking, and couldn't talk sensibly. He immediately ordered all the bottles and the glasses taken away, and forbade me from taking even a single drop of wine.

When I returned to my senses, I related to him in detail, the cause of my distraction and drunkenness. He sympathized with me, accompanied me day and night, and after a couple of days, took me to Paris. My grief and despondence eased with the change of atmosphere and the lively clubs of Paris. I regained my mental and physical health in about a month, and we reached Cambridge as the vacation ended. I returned to my books and to my academic activities.

Gentlemen, three years have passed since the mysterious and besetting incident occurred and jolted my life, and I haven't yet completely forgotten her! I have been always visualizing her dancing figure, since my arrival here. I feel, I can't quite forget Isabella. You've once again made me restless by making me recount her story. Dry, healed wounds have once again started opening. Please allow me to leave now! I can't stay here any longer. Bye!"

Rafiq finished his story and got up to leave. We were all surprised and speechless, lost in his passionately overwhelming tale.

He was right at the door, when Mahmoud called him, "Rafiq sahib, you've promised to tell us about the five challenging and unanswerable questions your story poses! We want to know them."

"O really, I'm sorry! I was so agitated, I couldn't remember that. Listen, the thing that puzzles me first is that how the identity of Isabella was related to that of the parrot and the picture in the frame. Secondly, how I being a philosopher and a rationalist, fell in love with a phantasmagorical figure. The third riddle was Miss Isabella herself. How the heavens the fascinatingly beautiful figure was transformed into a real young woman in flesh and blood. The fourth incredible thing is that why the picture of the parrot vanished after the death of Miss Isabella? Bye, bye gentlemen! Hope to see you again!"

As Rafiq was half way out of the door, I exclaimed, "Rafiq . . . what about the last point, the fifth one?"

"I'll tell that later! No hurry!" Rafiq answered, smiling.

"Oh, no! We want to hear it now. Please tell us before you go!" Amjad pleaded.

"Gentlemen, it's not so important! The last surprising thing is that I still don't understand how a dry man like me could relate such an excitingly fascinating story that bears no relationship with truth from the beginning right to the end." Rafiq laughed as he replied to me.

"What . . . what? Was the story totally false? Was it all a figment of your imagination?" Shakir asked nervously.

"Oh, yes, it was a completely tall and made-up story! It doesn't have to do anything with my past or present life. Okay gentlemen, I'm very busy! I've got to go to the theatre. It's already half past eight now. Thank you all!"

"Rafiq . . . Rafiq . . . hear me, please!"

But he was gone! My call returned unanswered. We were watching each other's faces, stunned and speechless.

References

1. betel leaf, prepared with betel-nut, and condiments etc. consumed in India and Pakistan.
2. a game resembling the game of checkers or draughts, played in India in olden days

10. SEA AND THE SKY

Ghyas Ahmed Gaddi

Her eyes scanned the room as she entered. Nothing had changed. The thin paint on the walls, glazed doors, window curtains fluttering as the wind caught them, the old dressing table, the bed, the sofa, and her father's twenty years old portrait hanging on the wall, of a man with an impressive face, lively bright eyes, and broad forehead. Everything was the same as she had left them three months ago.

With an overwhelming feeling of love and respect she silently made her salaam to the man in the picture.

Ever since she grew up, Kala, driven by an obsessive fascination, had been privately saluting, like an arcane ritual each morning, the handsome man whose picture was hanging on the wall. He was her own father, the first man that Kala saw as she opened her eyes to the world. A strange bond existed between them. She didn't feel comfortable till she took her evening tea with him, or made up his bed with her own hands. She felt woefully incomplete unless she read aloud Ghalib's verses or Kabir's couplets to her father till late night.

Leaving even her important chores aside, she would continue sitting and talking with her father till he drifted off to sleep. And then she would get up, plant a soft kiss on his forehead, and looking around inadvertently towards the door, leave the room.

A strange sensation came over her, every time she kissed her father. *Why does it happen? What pushes her to kiss her father? And even if she does that, why is it that she casts furtive glances around the room after doing so?* She searched inside her mind for answers. But she did not have to dig deep for any. *He was her father, after all.* Her inside responded.

She often declared openly to her father, "O babuji, you're so lovely! I can't live without you. I don't why I feel like that. Can you tell me why?"

Bursting into laughter, her father would embrace her and say, "It's because I'm your father!"

On such occasions her mother always entered the room, protesting vigorously, "Well . . . well, am I no one to you then? Why doesn't the girl love me? She never comes forward to hug me so fondly."

"The reason is that Kala is her father's daughter, and not her mother's. You're Inder and Sita's mother not . . ." Her father quipped, laughing.

It was then that Kala realized the veracity of her mother's complaints against her. True, the desire to ask her mother for things had never risen in her. She always turned to her father for her needs, though Inder and Sita often clung closely to their mother's arm. *Why couldn't she do the same?* It appeared to her that she was really her father's daughter. Her mother had given birth to her, and that was the only bond that linked them.

Her mother, quite naturally, was the first woman that she saw at her birth. She never liked her though. She could clearly imagine her as a shabbily dressed, unattractive woman, with a drawn face, dishevelled hair, sunken cheeks, and lifeless eyes. How mean she looked in front of her father! Her mother's hideousness led Kala to believe that women were decidedly inferior to women. Her belief strengthened as she grew to maturity.

And men . . . . Her father epitomized the image of man in her mind. Kind, caring, dignified, and handsome, he embodied for her ultimate male superiority. That was the reason why she loved her brother Inder more than her sister Sita. She liked playing carom with him all through the day, and completely ignored her mother's insistent summons to help her in kitchen or Sita in her studies. She felt she just couldn't give them a hand. But she willingly tutored Inder, changed his clothes, and kissed his forehead.

She always felt a strange pleasure in spending long hours with him. Inder's broad forehead looked a lot like their father's. But the image of man that endured in her conscious mind illumined the picture of only one person—her father. She loved him, revered him, as she did his mirror image Inder, her younger brother. She carried him on her back all day long, the boy's arms girdling around her neck, till she heard the sound of heavy shoes. She would then dismount Inder with rare quickness and rush down the stairs, the nearing footfalls filling her with delight.

"Babuji . . . !" She would gleefully exclaim on catching sight of him.

Smiling affectionately, resting his hand gently upon her shoulder, the man would climb up the stairs to his room.

The evening sky had now darkened. Breaking the spell of memory, Kala went into the balcony, grasped the balcony rail, and looked out on the street. The streetlights had already come on. She knew not how long she stayed there. Mornings mellowed into afternoons, and afternoons darkened into evenings as time rolled on. Unable to seize the fleeting movement of time, Kala cried out loud, inside her. *'What has befallen me . . . ! Why to me . . .'*

But her aural world lay still and silent, not even a footstep was audible. Distraught, she returned to her room, to the same walls, the same windows with iron grills. She was tired of her clichéd little prison world. She wanted to escape it but . . . *However the borrower tries to flee away, the lender doesn't allow him that freedom until he squeezes out his last penny from him.* She was getting fed up with a world that demands a heavy price for what it gives, that feeds on creating differences, divisions.

Kala walked slowly to the other corner of her room. Light filtering out of the next room, reminded her of the gloom that had set in her own world. She wished to turn the light on, but stopped.

The next moment she stepped out of her room and tiptoed towards the other room, whose inside was hidden behind a drawn velvet curtain hanging across the door, which, however, couldn't stop from escaping out the faint voices of her mother and Sita. Inder had just left the room next to it with a racquet in his hand.

For full eleven days, eleven long nights, she had lain incarcerated in her room like a prisoner, and never once did Sita come to see her, nor even her darling brother Inder cared to take a peep. Her mother, however, taking heavy steps came for a while, looked at her sadly, and left hanging her head like a culprit. She looked at the heavy, drawn curtain hiding her mother's room from view. *Hadn't the coloured curtain become still heavier? Couldn't she pull it back and go behind it?* Kala said inside her head.

And suddenly her steps quickened. *'I'm going to raise the curtain. My arms are still strong.'* But the moment she touched the it, her entire body numbed, her hands trembled with fear.

"What's it, Kala? Do you need anything?" She could clearly recognize her mother's voice.

Kala realized she had lost something, there was something missing in her which she urgently needed to redeem.

"Shall I get you tea?"

"Oh no mama, no . . . !" She noticed a strange kind of love in her mother's voice. A love so deadly, so unintelligible! She doubted whether she was really her mother. Tears streamed from her eyes.

"Hasn't daddy yet . . ." her voice quivered.

"Your father has started coming late these days, when it grows pitch dark. Although he leaves his office early, God knows where . . ." She could clearly notice a sort of suspicion in her mother's voice. It pierced through her heart like a spear.

Kala became restless at her mother's irreverence for her father. *How could mother say that? How dare she abuse daddy like that? Why was she so insulting? She had never asked her mother to call her back after she had run away from the house. Was she forcibly brought back only to hear indecencies uttered against her daddy?*

She felt like fighting with her mother, scratching her face for sending her gangster brother to snatch her out of Sudhir's embrace, and bring her back to the house.

The thought of Sudhir filled Kala with dread. He suddenly appeared on the horizon of her mind. *Did Sudhir survive the dagger attacks of the goons? Who knows Sudhir's body might be rotting on the rocks of Mahabaleshwar!*

Her eyes moistened. A seething pain lanced through her body and went deep inside.

Sudhir . . . dear Sudhir! Why can't I forget you?

She came back to her room and got into her bed. The wound on her wrist was healing. Kala couldn't see it in the darkness of the room, but started rubbing the fainting scar softly. The scars were healing in barely eleven days.

Some more days will pass away and then perhaps you will be completely forgotten.

She was momentarily startled by the sound of Sita's raucous laughter coming from the curtained room. Her first impulse was to ask Sita the reason for her mirth, the other to request her to include her too in that happiness. But she resisted both. It was almost ages since she had laughed heartily. Sita was laughing again, but not alone. This time her mother had also joined her. And Kala . . . , bereft of any merriment any joy, was standing utterly alone, far away from her mother and her sister.

A bitter smile played on her lips. Perhaps her mother was taking her revenge on her for an old grudge. She had never turned to her mother, never cared for her. And she also knew fully well that her vengeful mother would make her account for every bit of disdain with which she had been treating her.

Well done, mother! Keep laughing, why should you care even if I die someday? She said silently.

Suddenly Kala climbed out of her bed, wiping her wet eyes. She cheered herself up and began pacing slowly around the room. Wandering in the shadowy room like a lost traveller, she stopped a while, and looked out of the window. Utter darkness beyond petrified her with fear, quickening her heartbeat. She closed the window instantly as if barring the darkness from entering the room.

Groping her way in the pitch-black room, she felt the light switch on the wall, and flicked it on, bathing the room in a silver light. The object that first caught her eyes in the brightness was the framed photograph of her father's sitting on the side table.

'*Babuji . . . full eleven days have passed and I haven't had a glimpse of you.*' Her lips quivered releasing soft voices, and her eyes brimmed with tears.

How pitiless you are, babuji! Where is your tender loving care when I need it most? A friend and yet not standing by me when I'm distraught! I need the warmth of your comforting hands, my dear babuji. I've come back lonely and friendless except you in this dark world and wide. I regret at not having listened to you, and now beg you to treat me with the same compassion and love that you once showered on me. How can a friend like you become so stony and unfeeling, dear babuji?

Kala wept silently, uncontrollably, unaware of the passing time, and when finally she recovered herself it was past midnight. The night was unduly long and tough as the winding, rugged mountain path. Time was dragging terribly for her. She got out on to the balcony. Black ominous clouds had darkened the sky above, throwing deep sinister shadows all around.

A faint smile flickered across her face. It displayed her confidence that however heavy and fitful the night was, it had to fade far away, replaced by the bright daylight. And the day would pass as had those eventless eleven previous nights and days without heralding any change in her circumstances. The dance of light and darkness went on its usual course, but her grim, unhappy fate remained unaltered. That was the only truth that had forced itself on her.

Kala mind was shuffling between hope and despair. Lost in thoughts she wondered whether the dull roots of her life could be ever stirred with spring rain.

Was that also true that her parents who had brought her to the world were the only arbiters of her destiny? She had quarrelled with them, had disallowed the tender passionate paternal love to go along with those intense, genuine feelings which appeared so true and overwhelming, like the pulsating beats of life.

Wasn't it true that her parents had forcibly snatched her out of the passionate embrace of her beau? She and her distraught swain cried for one another at the foot of the hills of Mahabaleshwar, pleaded desperately not to be ripped away from one another, banged their heads in despair. It dawned on them that day that their love would never be allowed to flower. He was cut off from her and perhaps from his own life. She had to return to her prison hole, alone.

She had no knowledge what happened to Sudhir after that incident. Suddenly, a pain shot through her heart, and wounding her entire being, disappeared somewhere. She looked up at the dark sky, and down to the plants and flowers which were bathed in darkness like her own fate. Something burnt within her, and a sharp voice echoed from the innermost recesses of her heart like the sharp, shining blade of a knife.

She too should have left the world with him.

Kala returned to her room, turned off the light and got into her bed. Her gloom subsided after a while, overtaken by her conscience which exhorted her to think and act sensibly. *I am still alive and I have to face the reality that I have compromised with life, and am going to resign to my fate for the rest of my life. That's the ultimate truth.*

She suddenly felt inclined to believe that love only sought itself to please. For her, love was as self-seeking as it had been since a thousand, a million years ago. The thought bewildered her, and she closed her eyes. And there he was before her closed eyes, looking strangely feeble and sinewy. She felt as if she had secured Sudhir behind her closed eyelids.

I've shielded you from any harm, Sudhir. Be happy wherever you are! May you glow with so much happiness that the world learns it from you. Kala's thoughts were laced with burning passion. Fresh hot tears fell from her eyelids and were swallowed by the darkness of the night.

Eleven days and eleven waking nights! Time flies like gusts of wind, leaving behind, as it passes, blurred footprints down the mists of memory. It never looks back. The ocean of time is vast, endless. Our lives, like tiny waves roll out of its depths, and flow down to the farther shore, breaking on it, annihilating as they hit it.

Time is beyond measure. Kala thought and as she did her head pounded. She sighed and rubbed a hand across her forehead. A weak smile escaped from her lips. Time's ocean is limitless, and the waves that do not break billow wildly on the crest of water, like roving lunatics. Time never stops nor does it let others rest in peace even for a moment. Was he too swept away by the running stream of time or swallowed by thc rogue waves? Sudhir . . . the fulfilment of her dreams, the reason for the raging sea within her; whose love was like the infinite expanse of the azure sky!

The smile that played on her lips betrayed anguish not mirth. Her conscious, rational mind suddenly began to wander. *All these are words, mere words. They are meaningless in the absence of feelings and emotions. However distinct they appear, they are dependent on each other. Words lose their veracity if they do not carry feelings. The emotions that rise in the heart like enormous tidal waves, like deadly tornadoes, like dancing orgies of demons, lie inside, smothered and stifled without the aid of words. The more they are left unexpressed the more fiercely intense they grow.*

Kala felt her eyes. They were streaming. The rising waves had broken on the edges of her eyelids, and were rolling slowly down her cheeks. A sharp pain hit the middle of her chest, and her lips quivered with emotion. Pressing her lips between her teeth, she gently touched the tender spot. It ached like the sharp stab of knife. Her effort to shore up a smile brought warm drops falling from her eyes, as if the wounded heart was bleeding out. She had so much to say, but in the absence of Sudhir, she felt there was no one who would listen to her surging, pent-up emotions which threatened to rend her heart asunder. She was finding it extremely difficult to hold them inside. Her emotions rose like a whirlwind up inside her, and changed into tears when she failed to lace them with words. She needed words . . . words . . . in the absence of which her feelings were rambling within her, shaking her being.

Even if she had articulated her overwhelming feelings she had no sympathetic listeners. She wished to scream out her despair, her helplessness, but her inability to express herself was pinning her down. From where could she bring those words that contained the endless sea of her unbearable sufferings? But who could listen to her in that vast and wide world except . . . ?

Lying quietly in her bed, she looked at the picture frame, with her wet eyes. Her father's picture was drowned in the darkness of the room. Her compassionate father, a true friend, the beacon of light that had illuminated her life throughout her conscious existence, was now himself plunged in darkness. The ocean of time surged ahead roaring, wandering about, and was lost in the valley of darkness. Kala trembled with fear. The small room was sunk in deep gloom. The air outside had become still in the quietness of the garden, and darkness had spread all around like a contagious disease.

A sudden fear coursed through Kala. *Where was she lost in that threatening darkness? What place was that? Where was Sudhir? Her ship had sunk in the deep ocean of time. Nothing was visible. Not even the mast of the sinking ship. She tried to look all around her with her eyes wide open. She could see nothing. Only darkness. Her country, glittering splendidly in the golden lights of the Diwali lamps, appeared so dark and desolate as if it had been looted by a raiding pirate, or a greedy Ghaznawi, or plundered by the firangi coloniser.*

A searing pain rose from the depth of her heart and made her restless. *'O my Chishti! Where is your song that once enlivened India? My country is burning. Thick palls of smoke are rising and clouds of dust are swirling from all around. I've only tears left to shed. Be happy . . . ever . . . always.'*

She was suddenly startled. *Had she gone mad? Who was she talking to? There was nobody there, save the looming darkness, as far as the eyes could see. She stepped out slowly to the balcony. Nothing was visible. But then who was it? She had just felt somebody kissing her forehead. Where was that person lost? Where did he vanish behind the darkening folds of the curtains?*

The raging storm within her finally spent itself, and Kala somehow succeeded in containing the frantic rush of her thoughts. She realized, at last, that the ground beneath her feet was hard and real, and the sky above her was far away. There was not a soul near her, save an eerie stillness, a pervading gloom, and a stony, unending silence. Feeling desperately lonely, she impulsively walked out of her room, and found herself standing at the door of her father's bedroom. Her father was perhaps sleeping. The door was left on the latch, and the constant whirr of the ceiling fan inside was clearly audible in the silence outside. Soft green light was filtering out from the tiny crack at the bottom of the door.

Unintentionally, in a rush of unfathomable feelings, she gave the door a gentle push, and it opened with a slight creak. As she entered the room, her heart thumped heavily and then sank down. Tiny drops of sweat glistened on her forehead. A vague fear ran through her, combined with a strange sense of guilt, and disappeared as suddenly as it emerged. She lifted her eyes and saw her father sleeping deeply in his bed. In the green bedroom light, his ageing body lay still as if devoid of life. She went near him, and looked at him intently. Nagging worries had cast their terrible shadows on his face. She noticed some deep wrinkles there which she had never seen before.

An unknown fear compelled her to turn around and see if there was anyone else in the room, watching her. *But why should she care? What difference would it make even if anyone was watching her?* She failed to find an answer to her awkward question. The door on the left, which led to the room where his mother and Sita were sleeping, was open. She tiptoed toward it, and closed it quietly, quaking with fear of rousing them.

Kala returned to her sleeping father, and her eyes fell on his bare feet, as the sheet had slipped from over them and was hanging down from the bed. She picked up the sheet but something within her withheld her from covering the unconscious old man's bare feet. Putting the sheet aside, she fixed her eyes on them in the soft green light of the room. Her eye suddenly welled up. In the chilly wilderness of her heart, some comforting gusts of warm wind started blowing; the cloud of dust cleared from her memory, a strange pain awakened inside, and her eyes started shedding tears. Weeping quietly but copiously, Kala gently rested her quivering lips on the feet of her kind, compassionate old father.

"Who . . . who's that? Kala . . . you?" The old man woke up at the sound of her sobs and turned on the electric switch with the remote control on his bed, and the room was bathed in light. He tried to draw up his legs but stopped. He saw his daughter was clinging to his feet, weeping profusely.

He stretched out his arms and drawing her close to his chest, asked with passion in his voice, "Are you crying, my darling?"

Kala let out a shriek and hiding her face in her father's embrace, started crying like a child, "Forgive me . . . babuji! Please . . . !"

Her voice broke. Her father planted his lips on her forehead with sheer affection, and answered emotionally when he couldn't control his own tears, "Where had you gone, my child? How could you take such a silly step? Didn't you feel for a moment that you had an old father whose eyes must be searching around the world for you? And you left me alone!"

"You were looking for me?" Kala's voice broke with emotion and quavered as she looked up at her father's face with surprise.

"Why were you searching me, babuji?"

"Why shouldn't I, my dear? Every evening, after I returned from work, I'd sit late till midnight in the balcony looking out on the street. And at my office, I felt all day, during your absence, that you had come back home." He wiped her tears and then dried his own.

"How can you say that babuji? I've been here alone for eleven days, but you . . ." Kala asked, trying to control her surging emotions.

"I went to your room many times around midnight and found you relaxing in your armchair, looking out intently over to the garden outside, or sleeping quietly in your bed. Every time, I felt like spanking you for your defiance."

"Then why didn't you do that?" Kala looked lovingly at her kind father. "Punish me now, babuji! Hit me hard! I've hurt you too deeply!" She said, breaking down into tears.

They stayed together for quite some time, until all their pains and sufferings were washed away with their tears. Her father picked up his cigar from the side table and pressing it between his lips lighted it.

He then removed her gently from his hug and asked, "Would you make me some coffee, my child? Look there! The coffee maker and the coffee box are there on the corner table. I brought my coffee things in my room after you left. Who else would I ask for a coffee?"

Kala got up, arranged her hair, and turning her eyes towards her father, answered, "Sure, babuji! I'll go and make some now."

When finally she brought him coffee, her father asked, "What about you, my child?"

"Thanks babuji! I don't have any appetite!"

"Really . . . ? Fine, then I too ain't going to have it!" He looked at Kala, and patting her head with utmost affection, cheered her up, "Forget what had happened, my child. Leave living in the past now. Consider it strongly that you are going to start a new day in your life from tomorrow. You're not going to lock yourself up in your room, and I'll stop going out at daybreak and coming back late at night. If someone stumbles on a rock and falls down, he starts making bad faces, and the world laughs at him. But if the man shores up courage, stands up and starts walking confidently, the world doesn't look back at him."

Kala listened to him quietly bowing her head.

He held her chin and lifting her face, said, "My daughter is going to walk with her head raised from tomorrow. She isn't going to bow before anybody, because her father is going to be with her, always."

Kala stared at her father with passionate love and gratefulness. Tears fell from her eyes. But these were now tears of happiness, of love and thankfulness.

Outside, the earth and the sky had changed drastically, softening their terrible tempers, like newly melted candles, holding their breath, in absolute stillness.

11. SATYEN

Ilyas Ahmed Gaddi

Calcutta is an unexciting place. One can never find there the colour and the brightness that we usually see at the Connaught Place[1] *or Chaupati*[2]. I was tipped off by my colleagues when my forthcoming visit to Calcutta became office news. They informed me, perhaps as a word of caution that women in Calcutta do not move around displaying their bodies in funky, designer clothing. They, however, possess a tender and kind heart that aches even when it is even slightly hurt. And their eyes are extremely dark and sad, as if they are always on the alert against an unknown fear, like the eyes of a deer.

When I finally reached Calcutta, an old rickshaw puller took me to my destination. I was greeted at the door by a lively young girl. Though she wasn't very beautiful, her eyes were extremely attractive, very dark and deep, like the *Padma*[3] River.

She closed the door as we entered a small, windowless room, and sat beside me on an old, rather worn couch.

"Would you like some drink?"

"No, nothing!"

"Not even the imported?"

"No! I don't drink alcohol!"

"Really!" astonished at his answer, she continued, "But you must have some liquor here. I mean, to come here you have to stoop to the level from where monkeys had started evolving into humans."

"Oho! But actually, I'm in search of that lofty height from where man had started acquiring sainthood."

She gave a short, amused laugh, "You've come to the wrong place, then."

"Well, sometimes you go the wrong way and reach the right place! Don't you?"

"O yes! It's quite possible here, in Calcutta. I've often watched people going the right way but reaching the wrong place, here."

"You sound sensible enough! What's your name?"

"May name? O, they're many! Call me by any name! It hardly makes a difference."

I could not appreciate her casual manner. She too missed to understand my feelings that had brought me to the place. Perhaps she could not. I expected more from her, but she had decided to offer me as much as she was paid for, like a miserly grocer.

"Can you dance?"

"Why?" She appeared startled, but spoke cheerfully, "What do you want me to do? Have you come from the groom's side to decide on me?"

"Do you really feel any urge to marry?"

She appeared to be terribly embarrassed at my awkward question, but quickly controlled herself and replied, "No, never! Isn't marriage also a kind of trade?"

"Maybe for you! But I consider it as a spiritual bond!"

"Then what do you have to say about the relationship that has just now been established between you and me?"

It was not easy for me to answer her.

Finding me speechless, she burst into laughter.

"We've had enough of discussions! Come on, let's have some tea now. It has no alcohol." she said, getting up and moving towards the door.

"O thanks! I know well, what contains alcohol, and what doesn't!" I shot back.

She looked around at me, and smiled. I could not fail to notice a playful glaze in her eyes.

"Do you really?" She again exploded with laughter.

She called someone out to bring tea and returned to her seat.

"I don't mean to offend you! I'm sorry, I get moody at times! In fact, I want to come closer to people, but they never think about things beyond their needs."

"What about yourself . . . ?"

"O well, I always do, otherwise, till now, I would have lolled on the bed. And after that I wouldn't have remained my own self. I'd have changed into another woman. The funniest thing is that all those who visit this place, come looking for this another woman. No one comes for me!"

"Well, then I've come for you!" I said, tapping at my chest.

"Have you really? I'm not sure. Listen, why don't you stop pretending now? I know you're faking your feelings." There was an obvious mix of humour and irony in her voice. Her laughter was youthful and attractive, but her eyes were still sad and sunken. They sparkled when I spoke and then darkened, as when a glow-worm emits a shining light in the darkness of night, or a beam of light escapes out of thick clouds, for a while, and then complete darkness stretches away into the distance.

"Why don't we have some tea, and move out for a walk? We'll have dinner at the Royal, and then I'll leave you back here!"

"Oh no, sir! It's not so easy here! There are lots of people around who know me very well. I wonder what they would say if they see me with you!"

"Why do you bother yourself so much about the onlookers?"

"Why not? Do you take me to be a woman in the street? I have my house here, my relatives, my brothers and sisters. They all are under the impression that I'm a working woman."

"O, then you mean . . ."

"Well, well, I'm not alone doing that. There are countless girls in this town who are doing this, in the guise of working on jobs."

"But I've heard that girls here do not have bodies. I mean they don't display their physical aspect."

"You've been misinformed. Here women have nothing to show except their bodies. And not only women, it holds equally true in the case of men too. You may consider this town as a big oil-press into which hundreds of bodies are thrown. The oil-press churns and crushes them the whole day, and after squeezing all their spirit throws them back by the evening. The oil that runs the tube lines, burns the street lamps, and glitters the magnificent, towering buildings . . ."

"Hello, hello? Are you okay?" I clapped my hands. She looked startled and blushed crimson with embarrassment. The flush of anger that had glowed her nut brown complexion, suddenly vanished.

"Listen, darling!" I said, lifting her chin, "A beautiful girl like you should not utter such discouraging words. You should talk about flowers, stars, the moon, and the blessed easterly breeze, blowing at the unearthly hours of the night. So that when somebody suddenly comes before you and looks at your delicate face and glittering eyes, he would be obliged to ask you, '*What's thy name, O moon goddess*!'"

She broke into laughter, "Stop your sweet talks! They can never compel me to go out with you."

She kept on declining my request and I persisted with it, until eventually she agreed after prolonged argument, not on dining at any hotel, but on taking a round of *Dharamtala*[4] and back.

The streets were teeming with traffic, and the footpaths were buzzing with a flood of pedestrians scrambling around, with careless indifference, not even noticing their fellow passers-by. The girl's fear was absolutely pointless. Who, after all, was going to recognize her in the milling crowd?

But she was eventually spotted. This happened when I was taking her, against her wishes, to a clothes store, to get her a blouse piece. A young boy of about sixteen was standing on the stairs of the shop. He looked miserable—crumpled half shirt, a scruffy pair of jeans, unkempt hair, strangely stretched eyes. We had reached to the shop doorway when she saw him. Their eyes met for a moment before she quickly turned hers away.

The girl's hand trembled in mine, and she held it tight, whispering into my ears, "Let's go back now! Quick!"

"But your clothes . . . ?"

"No, no leave it! We'll get it from another shop!" She started pulling me, and turned back to see the boy, who had melted in the surging crowd.

"Why, what happened?" I was surprised to find her so agitated.

"Oh, it was he . . . Satyen!"

She did not stop after that. I tried hard to buy her anything on our way back, or at least have some snacks, but she was in such a great haste and anxiety that it was impossible to mollify her.

After returning to her room, she drank water from the *surahi*[5] sitting on a tripod, and sank down into the sofa.

"I told you not to take me there . . . !"

"But what happened? Who was he?"

"He was Satyen, my younger brother. I'm very afraid of him."

"Why? Does he fight with you?"

"No, no, he doesn't. And that's exactly why I fear him. I want him to fight with me, hit me, abuse me, but he does nothing of that sort. He remains obstinately silent, and just keeps staring at me. And God forbid! How dreadful are those eyes! They seem to penetrate my body. I feel as if all its blemishes and blots are exposed to them, and I'm being stripped naked before him. A fit of anger seizes me then, and I start scolding him for abandoning his studies and wandering out with depraved street boys of the locality. But he doesn't say anything in reply. Only smiles. You know, it is that smile, that scornful, mocking, and hateful smile, you just can never imagine, that infuriates me."

"Renu . . . ! It's all your illusion or your brother's frustration. Find a job for him and a nice wife too! And that's all!"

"Well, he he'd been asked to marry, though he's not of a marriageable age, but he declined. In fact, he'd made friends with a girl who lived in our neighbourhood. Both studied together, and everyone around knew they liked each other. Perhaps, they were in love too. But slowly and silently he withdrew from her into his own world."

"That's not strange, my dear! Everyone pulls himself out of his obsessions, anyway. One day, you'll also withdraw from me!" My playful humour startled her back to her present world. Her eyes suddenly alighted with emotion.

"You're talking nonsense. In fact, it's the opposite. It's you who is going to withdraw. To tell you the truth, you men turn your back to the shore and walk away. Try, once at least, to go down the sea, and see how tumultuous it is."

"But what if you set me afloat?"

"Even if I do that, you'll float with me. I'll not break away from you. I shall hide you in my heart."

I was shocked. Sometimes, while moving with life, we unwittingly touch the most delicate part of other's hearts.

Her name was Renu Majumdar, and I had retained her for a month for two hundred rupees. She agreed to spend two days a week with me. That meant eight meetings. I was on a month long official visit to the city. There was no other solution for my loneliness in that bustling place. I expected her to be a good partner. She was not yet trodden on. There was, undoubtedly, something bright and lively within her that shone out brilliantly but briefly at times. I wanted to see that light very closely. I wished to touch it . . .

I met Satyen too during my stay there. Once when I was opening the door lock of my room, someone called me out from over my back, "Do you have a match box, please?"

I turned around, and lo, Satyen was standing there right in front of me. I stood amazed for a few moments. His face stiffened when he saw me. He, however, took the match box I was extending towards him, lighted his cigarette, and returned the match box immediately.

"Do you recognize me?" I asked him with extreme politeness.

He didn't reply immediately, but paused for some time, looked at me intently, and then said, "O yes! You're the fellow I saw the other day with *didi*[6]."

His tone was extremely offensive, like the hiss of a snake.

Satyen came to visit me a week after our first meeting. He looked rather happy. He was dressed in clean clothes, and the rigidness in his face had also softened. He had a suitcase in his hand, as if he was going out of the city, on a journey.

"*Dada*[7], would you mind my staying with you for the night?"

"Of course not! I'll be most happy! Are you travelling out?"

"Yes, but only for two days!" he said, putting his suitcase on the floor.

"Haven't you fought with *didi*?"

"Oh no, never! Why should I fight with her?"

He heard me with a partly sour partly sweet smile playing on his face.

"*Didi* is afraid of herself!" He replied promptly, and continued, "I love her the most. And she thinks nobody knows what she's been doing. When she leaves her room, with all her adornments, a strong gust of fragrance enters my room too. She goes away, and I keep guessing about the places where she'd be distributing that fragrance! When she comes back late at night, I try searching for the fragrance in her. That's the moment when she starts fearing, not me, but her own self. And then the entire defensive wall of adornment and fragrance that she had built around herself, starts crumbling down, without even a push. She glances at me, and rushes headlong into her room. But I don't say anything to her, because I know she is innocent."

I didn't realize he could think so deep. He looked too young for such profound thoughts. The hair on his face had just started growing. The sweet innocence that fades with age was still playing brilliantly on his face.

I asked him humorously, "How old are you, Satyen?"

"I'm sixty!" was his off the cuff reply.

"You mean sixty years?"

"Yes, I'm sixty years old!" He replied painfully. "There are no young men in this city. Down here, we enter the boundaries of old age the moment we cross the limits of childhood."

His reflection appeared very interesting. I held his hand in mine, and said, "Come with me to Delhi, Satyen! I'll get you a very good job there!"

"But *dada*, do you have a river there that flows just sometimes, and not always?"

I looked at him, surprised, and he laughed, "Leave it! You can't understand all this, in fact, no outsider can. This is something very important. Just ask *didi*!"

I never got an opportunity to put Satyen's query to her. When she came the next day to me, she looked extremely disturbed. She entered my room and slumped into the chair.

"Satyen is missing since yesterday!"

"Come on, now! Is that the only cause of your distress? He was with me last night, and went away just a few hours ago. He left telling me that he'd come back after a couple of days."

She appeared a bit relieved.

"But where has he gone?"

"He didn't tell me that!"

"Was there nothing with him?"

"No, he was carrying a suitcase!"

"Oho . . . !" She shivered, and then became silent. It appeared as if she was plunged into darkness. Her face turned pale.

"Did he fight with anyone in the house?"

"No!" She got up and started pacing restlessly to and fro.

"Some day . . . some bad news . . . ! Oh my God! I haven't yet prepared myself for that news! How can I bear hearing it?"

"But why are you so worried, Renu? Is he in any danger?"

"Oh, you don't know! He . . . he's very much here! In this very city!"

"What, here?" I was stunned.

"Do you have any idea what he was carrying in his suitcase? Explosives. He had explosives there. He delivers them—from one place to another."

"Oh, no!" My whole body trembled with fear.

Someday . . . some fateful day! O my God, how long can he go on escaping?"

She began crying bitterly. I watched her silently, like a mute ghost. All the gilt and embellishments of that playful, wanton girl of yesterday had been washed out from her visage and form. Outside, the rattle of the electric trams, blaring horns of the passing cars, and the rumbling sounds of the double-deckers, were echoing in the atmosphere.

References

1. officially *Rajiv Chowk*, is one of the largest financial, commercial and business centers in Delhi.
2. is one of the most famous public beaches adjoining *Marine Drive* in the *Girgaum* area of Mumbai, India.
3. The *Padma* is a major trans-boundary river in Bangladesh. It is the main distributary of the Ganges which originates in the Himalayas.
4. *Dharmatala* is a neighbourhood in central Kolkata, in the Indian state of West Bengal. It is a busy commercial area that had come up with the growth of Calcutta during the British Raj and is thus one of the repositories of history in the city.
5. a long-necked earthen goblet with a big round belly.
6. term of addressing the elder sister.
7. term for addressing the elder brother.

12. THE EVE-AFFLICTED FALCON

Devendra Issar

He came every Sunday, when the sun started sinking, its light falling off to disappear; and when the lengthening shadows of evening started gathering into darkness, as night stalked the place.

He would emerge, walking along the confluence of darkness and light, and enter the room, treading on the shrinking sunbeam falling on the half-open door.

He always entered without knocking at the door. He walked slowly into the room, creating a strange music by pressing a rolled leaf between his lips, blowing air through the hole, and stood right in front of the bed where a child lay flat motionless, but alive. He often touched his face softly with a flower petal, bringing it closer to his nose. Colour, touch, and fragrance, perhaps, produced tiny tremors in the child's body.

The kid could neither speak nor hear, ever since he was brought there a year ago. He could only see, lying quietly on his bed, like the dried trunk of a tree. But the moment he stepped in, it seemed as if light rain drops began to spray the dried trunk.

Whenever he came, he looked different, and he changed the child too into something new, something different. The first time that he came, he looked terribly old, miserable, and weary. He had the child in his arms, besmeared with blood, singed with petrol, diesel and acid. The child's body bore scratch marks like those that are made by finger nails, teeth, or iron nail. He rested the child softly on the bed, washed his wounds, dressed them, changed his clothes, wiped his face with his handkerchief, straightened out his hair, and kissed his forehead.

And that is how he started his treatment, which hardly affected the child. The child had no sensations except for the vision in his eyes. He, nevertheless, kept talking to him as if he was hearing everything, understanding all.

He always brought something new for the child, stood beside his bed, stroked his cheeks, and combed his hair. The child's lips quivered gently, but no voice escaped them. His eyes always sparkled with such brightness as if his whole body was speaking through it. And then, darkness would spread all around, encircling from all sides, like the ominously murky and desolate wilderness of the dense African jungle.

He would park himself on a stool, drawing it beside the child's bed, and tell him stories old and new—fairy tales of different countries, tales of beasts and birds, and sometimes of humans. He also used sounds and gestures to communicate his stories.

On his first visit, he had nothing but only this child in his arms. The second time, he came with a single-stringed harp in his hands. He sat facing the child, and played the harp for a long time. God knows what old forgotten notes he played on! They were very old film songs—sweet and sad—full of love and pain. The young boy blinked rapidly, expressing his pleasure. The musical waves of the harp seemed to course through the veins of his senseless body, like fresh, pellucid, warm sunrays. And it appeared as if, sailing on the tunes of the harp, he had started flying around the room like a bird, his body transformed into cotton flakes, floating in the air.

Then one day, he brought masses of flowers, soft and silky, of various hues, violet, azure, lilac, red, white, yellow, all having their own distinctive fragrance, with leaves of many shades of green. There were roses of many shades—red, white and black. He touched the sprawling young boy's body with those flowers. Fragrance, colours, and touch combined to create movement in the kid's body. He spread the flowers on his bed, and flew a seven-coloured butterfly in the air. It flew, dancing around the kid's body, fluttering along the bed, before his eyes, now whizzing out from the window, now flying in, scattering colours in the room.

And that very day, he planted a black rose in a small glass vase, and asked me to water it every day, and to keep it out sometime, so that it got fresh air and the brightness of the sun. I followed his instructions. Every day, without fail, I left the plant out in the veranda and sprinkled water on its leaves. The water drops dallied, and broke on the leaves, leaving them shining like a mirror. He sometimes applied manure to the soil. Slowly, the roses started blooming, opening their buds, spreading their aroma, and smiling. The child's eyes rolled with excitement; his lips moved. Perhaps he was also blossoming along with the roses.

Once he came with a show box. He called it a *bioscope*. We made such *bioscopes* in our childhood, by cutting out pictures from newspapers and magazines. We strung them together in sequence of pearly black and white pictures. Drilling two holes on each side of the show box, we fixed two reeds into them, and wound the reel of pictures on the reeds. Turning the reeds round with both hands, we would then watch the pictures through a glass that we fixed on the lid of the box, by making a round hole there. The pictures filled us with wonder, at how the world that appeared so big, had contracted into that little box in our house.

The picture world of the *bioscope* was full of innumerable birds, animals, insects, trees, rivers, waterfalls, seas, mountains, forests, villages, town, fields, flowers, fruits, vegetables, foods, and musical instruments; peoples in clothes of different colours, dancing, fighting, worshipping, carving figures of animals, birds, gods, goddesses, humans and weapons on walls of caves. Many, many centuries were rolling in that small box! Histories, civilizations, nations, peoples all came to life.

He set the *bioscope* near the young boy's face and rolled down the pictures, one by one, telling stories with each of them. This went on for a few days. He whirled him round, through antiquities of cultures, nations, religions, customs, traditions, and dances. Sometimes he played mouth organ, sometimes flute; sometimes he brought sweets, sometimes peacock feathers, and sometimes new cassettes. At times, he performed magic tricks before him, turning one ball into two, two into four. He occasionally formed changing patterns for him on a kaleidoscope, and drew strange silhouettes on the wall with his hands.

He kept on coming every Sunday, when the sun would start sinking, its light slipping down to disappear, and the lengthening shadows of evening spreading their darkness. He emerged, walking on the confluence of light and darkness. When the last ray of sunlight shrank, he would enter pacing on it, through the half-open door. He always went away as it darkened and lamps burned in the neighbouring houses, tearing the darkness down.

I always locked the door the moment he left, and peeped out sliding the windowpane a little. It was one such evening when, while I was looking out, my whole body stiffened and froze, and appeared to turn blue out of a growing fear of something weird and scary. And that very instant the ghastly spectacle was there before my eyes. My heart pounded, pulse rate quickened, and my blood congealed at the gory vision. I held my breath, as I looked towards the street.

What I saw was a large figure in ancient clothes, riding a chariot, drawn by wild looking horses, and followed by a huge crowd of screaming and shouting people. As the horses' iron shoes hit the metalled road, their friction caused spots of tiny sparks, as the horses galloped off. The horses' mouths belched black fire. Like a black serpent, the fire devoured everything that fell in its way. The chariot was made of gold, and its roof studded with precious jewels. The right wheel of the chariot left a trail of blood as it rolled on, and its left wheel a streak of fire. He rode on crushing all that met the wheels—children, men and women, young and old, birds, trees, plants all.

I never saw the charioteer's face, though he hadn't veiled it. I just couldn't see it. How could I recognize him? The chariot appeared to be the same every time, but perhaps the rider kept on changing. What I could remember well was only that the man's head was always crowned with shining coins, and those his chariot crushed were all bare headed, barely clothed humans.

It resembled the chariot that some years back had trampled the child who lay fallen under the wheels, spiked by the horseshoe nails. He was left there between the trail of blood and the streak of fire, until his benefactor lifted him in his arms, and brought him to my house. Since that day, the child had been in my care, lying down with deaf, mute and motionless, only looking in the empty space. The child's rescuer, his saviour came regularly every Sunday.

But one Sunday, quite unexpectedly, he didn't come. A few more Sundays passed, and he was still not to be seen. The child's eyes were glued to the door, where the sun's last rays slithered into the dark. The gleam in his eyes shimmered, as it fell on the spot that was gathering into darkness. It seemed as if his eyes were slowly losing their light. I shuddered with fear that he might lose his bond with the outside world. But perhaps his eyes had frozen on that spot.

When darkness started setting in the room, I quite habitually lighted the lantern, and occasionally checked out into the veranda, and on the road. I raised the wick of the lantern, and stayed waiting for him. The night had started growing thicker, heavier, darker, and longer. But he didn't come that night.

And then one day, he appeared, suddenly, when the sun had sunk, its evanescent light slithering to disappear; and when the spreading shadows of evening had already melted into darkness, not as before, out of the twilight. He walked directly into the room, quietly, from the half-open door, where the rays of light had disappeared sometime ago. He wasn't blowing any music with the tree leaf, when he entered. The night was pacing out step by step. Deathly silence had hung over the place that night—a silence eerier and deeper than the quarantined dense forests of Africa.

The charioteer had passed by the road moments ago. His chariot was, as usual, led by wild, sturdy horses. A huge crowd of people followed shouting and screaming. I had closed the windows and doors, when the chariot arrived. Suddenly, there was a knock on the door. Terrified, I opened the flap gingerly, and peeped out. It was him, the young boy's saviour. I opened the door, and he entered soaked in blood, scorched by acid, diesel and petrol.

His body bore gashes made by claws, nails, teeth and iron nails. His hairs were covered with dust, and his clothes were grimy with the grease of oil. The only distinctive feature in his whole body appeared to be his luminous eyes. He held a book in his hand. Its pages were torn, burnt, and drenched with blood. Every leaf of the book was soiled, and gave out the putrid smell of gunpowder. The book was worn out in many places, more than the wounds in his body. The words in the book had blackened. Smoke and the smell of gunpowder had smothered the room, as her entered it.

He stood in his peculiar way by the side of the bed, near the child. And then, pulling a stool by the bed, sat softly on it, and called me, "Mother, would you please bring the lantern nearer and raise its wick?"

He opened the burnt book with blood dripping from its pages, and started reading aloud. I asked him the name of the author, to which he replied, "He's a writer who can hear and speak but cannot see. And what I'm going to read now is a story about the last flower of the earth, the sole survivor . . ."

He then started reading aloud from the book.

"A terrible catastrophe had struck the world and annihilated the entire civilization. Towns, cities, villages, were all wiped out. The bushes and forests were all torched, and with them the gardens, groves and the well-preserved ancient artifacts. Men, women, children, the old and the young, and the animals, all started living a life worse than before. Hungry, frustrated dogs deserted their poor wretched masters in confusion, and strayed to strange places. Finding the dogs afflicted, even the rabbits attacked them. Books, paintings, music, vanished from the earth. Humans lay idle and helpless. Years upon years passed by. Those who were left alive forgot what they had achieved in the past through their sheer good deeds.

On reaching their adulthood, the boys and girls looked at one another with cold, expressionless eyes. Love had evaporated from this earth. But one day, the eyes of an adolescent girl who had never seen a flower, fell suddenly on one. It was the only remaining flower of the earth. She told the other humans that the flower was dying away.

Only one among the humans, a young boy who was wandering aimlessly, listened intently to what the girl had said. Both of them—the girl and the boy—watered the flower. They nourished it to blossom.

Then suddenly one morning, a moth appeared and started hovering around the flower. It hummed and hummed until it was not long before another flower appeared, and then four others, and then a host of them. Numberless flowers, trees, plants, bushes and forests, green and fresh, began to sprout. The young girl would sit near the flower, and watch it with excitement and pleasure. It was then that she felt the attraction and the fragrance of her body. The young boy realized how comforting the touch of her body was.

Love had again revived the world.

Their children grew into young men and women, beautiful and healthy. The dogs too came back from their exile. Young men started building houses of stones. Towns, cities and villages again came into existence and thrived, songs filled the air. People got down to making tools, weapons, musical instruments. Tailors, cobblers, painters, poets, sculptors and moneylenders all returned, as too the cruel soldiers and politicians, the allies and the adversaries, some here, some there. As days grew into months and months into years, they gradually drifted away from one another, until everybody started hating everybody.

And at last all that had happened before, happened again. Not once, but many times over. Every time the catastrophe was gorier, more dreadful, much more devastating than the one that had preceded it. Once again everything started perishing from the world. Only one man survived, with a woman, and a flower . . ."

He finished reading the story, and paused. The child's eyes had become glassy, staring unblinkingly in the void, as if waiting for him. They sparkled once, and then became lifeless.

He pulled out the flower, pressed between the pages of the book. It was drenched in the smoke of gunpowder, and was blackened by it. He washed it in pure, clear water, and placed it gently near the cheeks of the child. He then closed the book and walked out silently.

The story ends here.

Whenever the sun started setting, its light fleeting to disappear, and the creeping shadows of evening spreading into gathering darkness, a woman, heralding the prowling night, walked on the twilit gloom where the last rays of sun had begun to shrink. She would come out of the room through the half-open door, and in a fit of frenzy run blindly down the street.

The hapless woman is dead now. Her half-naked body is lying on the road. It is soaked in blood, singed with petrol, diesel and acid, and has deep gashes in her body as if torn by claws, nails, teeth, and iron nails. Her loose hair is soiled, and her clothes stained with grease. The only aspect of her that is obviously conspicuous is her eyes.

But look what's that! She lies there cold and lifeless, but clenched tightly in her fist, she is holding a flower, doused with the smell and smoke of gunpowder. It is a black rose—the earth's last flower.

13. ADAM'S BROOD

Khalida Hussain

The heavy whirling rotor blades of the helicopter, raising burning clouds of dry sand all around, had not yet halted to a stop. It appeared as if they didn't intend to cease spinning. They might actually have, but to him they seemed to be constantly whirling, unfolding in his mind the chain of events the disturbing memory of which had been besetting him of late—like the disconcerting image of an object that gets transfixed before the eyes for a long time.

He rubbed his eyes. They were full of flares. Sparkling embers of sand kindled everywhere between his palms and fingers and, in his nails, nose and ears. Stony dryness stretched everywhere and everything seemed to crackle. He tightened his toes inside his heavy boots. There was sticky moisture there. Its stink rose from the feet and landed in his throat. They had left him there, in the police jeep. He had turned police informer, and was helping them identify the terrorists. It was a Hobson's choice for him that though saved him his life, yet could do little to save him from his *benefactor's* wrath and abuses.

He saw all of them, all five of them, the inspector, the captain, and the three accompanying policemen, standing in a semi-circle near the helicopter. In the blackened sunshine of the strong summer heat, he tried to look with his eyes squinted, at the man who was emerging from the helicopter. The slim newcomer in army fatigues stepped out of the copter lifting his red blazing face in the scorching desert sun. His uniform, and his stout face and piercing eyes convinced him that he was from the army intelligence corps, a fact confirmed later.

After the exchange of salutes, they started walking in a group towards the waiting vehicles. They were now at such a distance from him that he could clearly see the intelligence officer's glassy blue eyes. They betrayed the place he was coming from. But were those eyes or marbles—cold, stony and expressionless? The man did not appear to have any distinctive quality for which he would be called on from overseas. When the entire group reached near the jeep, the intelligence officer glanced at him inquiringly.

Watching him looking thus, the inspector said, "Sir, he's our man."

And then twisting his mouth into a wry laugh continued, "He has rather been won over. People like him are very useful. We cannot manage without them.

Hadn't we found a few like him our job undoubtedly would have become very difficult, almost impossible."

The inspector was still under the impression that the intelligence officer did not understand their language correctly, though they had learned a few words of his language. These were enough, for everyday exigencies and, for serving their purpose. The intelligence officer, on the contrary, knew their language well, but apparently he did not want to reveal it to them. What sort of a language was it whose words rustled on lips like the sting of a hissing snake? Every instant a venomous taste filled his mouth.

They had got into the waiting vans now. He sat next to the driver while the inspector, the captain, and the visiting officer settled at the back seat, while the others took another waiting vehicle.

With a cigarette pressed between his lips, the officer asked the inspector, in a humiliating tone, "After all, what's going on in this part of the world? Aren't we disgracing ourselves on this cursed, ominous desert only to be maddened by them—the scum of the earth? There's something mysterious, some enormous diabolical power in them that just refuses to die. Aren't we sometimes haunted by dreams of people we had killed, but who don't just die with their death? After a few moments of dying, their ghosts again come back to life and rush to strangle us. Isn't this the desert's nightmare."

Sitting on the front seat, he had recognized the voice of the captain who was accustomed to kicking with his boots the groaning skeletons lying stretched in the prison cells.

He remembered how once in the midst of his savage operation, the captain, searching his pocket for a cigarette, had dropped his crimson wallet on the ground which flipped open displaying the picture of a blond girl with auburn hair, her mouth opened lasciviously, showing her blood red lips.

The captain had instantly picked up his wallet and started laughing recklessly putting his boots hard in the chest of his breathless captive, Abu Hamza, who was reclining on the heated wall of the cell. The now condemned Abu Hamza was once so healthy that everybody called him Hercules! But after he was wounded, captured and tortured in the cell, some poison had spread in his body, and he was transformed into a cudgel of bones in just a few days.

Memories raced through his mind as he was sitting silently and upright, all through the way.

"It needs skill to destroy that which makes man a human being. As long as you do not wipe out this human element, even the weakest man will make your life miserable. He'll make it hard for you to live, will make you mad." The intelligence officer declared, holding the cigarette in his mouth.

As the jeep reached the prison, two sentries on guard opened the huge metal gate, clicked their heels together, and saluted. The jeep stopped near the barracks. This time the inspector beckoned him, and he got down the jeep and stood right in the middle of all five of them.

The inspector was telling them, assuming he did not understand his language well, "He's very close to the rebels. We seized him luckily. He knows it's impossible to live without bread, and any price is too little to pay for breathing. Death is an extremely unbearable reality, nothing is so starkly, brutally real. He too is afraid of death, and therefore he's here. Keep a close watch on him! He is very useful for us as long as he's cooperating. You all know it is he who has informed us about the biggest gang of rebels . . . those vile b . . ."! He then spouted a filthy abuse.

"O Amin, may your parents mourn you! This slur is now your only reward, your identity." Voices were automatically swelling in his skull.

"O yes, he's. Isn't he?" The intelligence officer said, shoving his iron fingers into his chest. He staggered with the sudden thrust. Those standing around grinned.

"What's his name?" The officer's eyes were stony. His mouth appeared like a narrow crevice in the centre of a blue rock. Lips did not part when he spoke. Perhaps he always kept his teeth pressed together.

"His name's Amin. He was a university student and ring leader of a revolutionary group. The rest of them, by the way, are hanging about in cell number zero . . . zero . . . zero. You'll be happy to see them and commend us on our job."

The captain kicked him hard against the wall.

"That's okay! I want to start the job immediately. I've no time for talks", the intelligence officer said, moving fast ahead.

All five of them walked alongside him. The captain shouted at him as he moved on. Blood oozed out of the wound in his big toe and drenched his socks. Sharp stabbing pain shot through his legs up to the neck, like running electric current. A strange commotion raged spiraling in his stomach. Two full days had passed since he had had anything to eat or drink, and this was all because of that bridled captive, Abu Hamza.

Amin clearly remembered that fateful day when Abu Hamza, the now emaciated prisoner, was gearing up for a suicide attack. His accomplices Laila and Quddoos were also there. They were hiding in the small room of a dilapidated building, which was completely hidden from sight by a huge heap of debris surrounding it. After much effort, he had picked some mildewed crumbs of bread from the heap of garbage scattered around. Everyone in that little room was trying to peck at his share of crumbs.

Laila had a long deep cleft in her cheek. A shard of glass had stuck there. Abu Hamza pulled it out with his forceps. Laila's hands froze with excruciating pain and she was shivering. The same day her father and younger sister were driven to an undisclosed place, though they were in fact searching for Abu Hamza and Laila.

Branded as terrorists, residents upon residents were shoved into jails. Before this, they did not know that prisons were larger than habitations. No one, by the way, was allowed to go near them.

Abu Hamza took a pinch of the rotten bread in his mouth and vomited, "It is infested with worms. One should rather have a decent death than dying with bacteria."

Laila, at that moment, was tying the belt around her waist.

"But what will they or you yourself gain out of it? You don't even know who they are and how many. Some of those who are utterly inconsequential may get implicated in this explosion. And above everything else, your father and sister aren't going to gain anything from it." He had told Laila.

"They are not going to be benefited from anything now." Laila had replied.

"I know what Sakina would have suffered were she still alive, and my father . . ." She deliberately left the sentence incomplete.

"Do you wish what has befallen Sakina should happen to me too?"

"No, no." He had instantly replied, and then started setting the device right away.

Laila had appeared remarkably calm. He clasped her hands. They were gently warm. Her brown eyes appeared darker. He had blushed at his own actions and released Laila's hands. Unruffled, she started lighting her cigarette. She had got addicted to smoking since the beginning of her college days. Lounging against the wall, she sat on the floor calmly puffing at her cigarette with her eyes closed, sending out curls of smoke from between her fleshy lips. Abu Hamza hit the leftover piece of bread on the wall.

"It's entirely impossible to believe. The guy in shining armor emerges from a six feet deep underground hole like a rat, but fails to rescue us anymore. Amin, you don't have faith in heavenly powers! Do you? Would you still not believe that for centuries, Providence has been planning this for us. And centuries are not more than just a few seconds in His calendar. The blood of the innocent has been saturating this earth for ages. The curse cast on them is proving true word by word." Abu Hamza got up and started walking, if he could, in that little hole of a room.

"Abu Hamza! I'm surprised at you. How superstitious you are! You're a doctor, even then you believe in things like these. This is just trash. The whole world is brimming with innocent blood. This is human history. Who isn't cursed? After all, what else are blessings and curses?" He said peevishly.

"I too didn't believe that, but the wailing wind sweeping through the land has been a testimony to it. The land here may go on spewing out liquid gold. But nothing is going to change. Starvation and oppression have been forced like cloaks upon the generations here. Right now, the problem I'm faced with is concerned with registering only my share of protest by choosing a better way to die."

"But that's not necessary. It isn't necessary to die for that. Not at all! To keep living is more credible, more natural." Someone within him had said, and in utter confusion, he asked himself if that was courage or cowardice.

Abu Hamza's father was a farmer, and Leila's father worked as an oil driller. They were all hard-working people who knew how to endure physical suffering, who felt pleasure in toil and torment. On the contrary, he was the son of a professor who had spent all his life with books and words. He taught others the philosophy of life and logical determinism, but never got any opportunities to test it himself. All of it dissolved into his own blood.

Books turn people into cowards. He thought and felt mortified at his interpretation. Distant memories came flooding back in his mind. *'My father was a man of great refinement. He could not tolerate even a small speck of dust in the house. He used to walk barefoot on the marble floor of his room and the soles of his feet stayed spotlessly clean like those marbles. Everything in his room looked clean and glittered like glass.*

However, in his neat and tidy surroundings, he lived in constant fear of physical pain. Physical suffering and the thought of death always kept him terrified. For this reason alone he spent a good part of the closing years of his life in prayers and invocations.'

But he was different from his father. The terror of death and physical suffering was the only share of his inheritance. Apart from that, no beliefs and concepts had any relevance for him, except bare facts and matters at hand. Only they were real, nothing else was. He believed that existence meant nothing other than preserving one's body by any means, and all that man needed to strive for was to get rid of pains and sufferings. Pain, moreover, is a reality, sheer physical reality.

He remembered how Laila stood facing him. Her beautiful body, which he couldn't help touching, was shrouded in a black cloak. He knew she was engaged to Abu Hamza. That was one reason for his embarrassment. He felt as if shame and regret, instead of blood, were coursing through his veins.

Just then, Abu Hamza said, "Laila, you must reach at the crossing of the bank at five past ten and right at the same time, I'll get to the Market road."

He then, took out a small camera from his shirt pocket, and called Amin with the loving care that was reminiscent of the old times, "Amin, my angel! Take my snap and after my death send it to the media to show them how happy I was at that point in time."

Abu Hamza threw his arms round Laila, who lodged her head on his shoulder, her cheek touching his. He saw this clearly through the camera lens, and clicked. The two, then, walked quite slowly out of the small room. Outside, in the open, it was utter desolation. Dogs were biting into the heap of garbage in the distance, and airplanes were rumbling in the sky.

He stayed in that empty room until five past ten, leaning back against the wall at the same place where Laila was lying crouched some moments ago. Stubbed out cigarette ends lay on the floor before him; silvery brown ashes scattered around them. He got up exactly at six past ten, and went out. He hadn't gone far when suddenly he heard an explosion and his eyes fell on dismembered body parts flying in the air. When they landed on the ground he could recognize from the littered human debris the parts of Laila's beautiful body, and Abu Hamza's strong arms hanging loose by his sides and his broad chest dumped flat on the ground. He felt the pain, the torment, and the awe that a dying soul has to suffer.

He remembered Professor Abdul Hameed's lecture explaining the controversies on the definition of death. *'What, after all, is death? It is a reality, the bare truth. And, it is no story telling that it comes just the same way as when your clothes get tangled in a thorny acacia tree, and as you try to free them they are torn to pieces. Death tears life the same way. The clothes do not survive, but the acacia lives on. The acacia will continue living.'*

He listened to the sound of explosion in the air and raised his nose to smell gunpowder. Instead of the sound and smell of gunpowder, the air weighed with the thud of heavy boots, and the next moment he found himself surrounded by blown bits of weapons, and a posse of policemen.

Soon the cops pounced on him, kicked him savagely, and took him into captivity. His hands and feet were bound, and between torrents of filthy verbal abuses beyond his imagination, the police officer asked him,

"*Where are they? Where are the rest of them?*"

That was a nerve-racking experience for him. Undoubtedly, the ripping of skin, the pulling out of nails and, the crushing of tender parts of the body, were quite unjustified, as he had hardly anything to divulge. Undoubtedly, fresh bread and physical comfort are very necessary—the most necessary things. While entering the cabin, he had told the interrogator that both Abu Hamza and Laila were present at the crossing of the bank and the market at exactly five past ten. The cops discovered the camera reel from his trouser pocket. Laila's beautiful eyes and the touch of her soft warm hands came alive before his eyes. Continuous flow of tears unwittingly rolled down his cheeks and got mixed with putrid spit that was shot out at his mouth.

Laila had dissolved into the elements as if she had never existed. Abu Hamza, however, was picked up half-dead. Wounded people like him are extremely valuable in getting secrets uncovered, especially those who are morally weak like him.

"*Amin!*" He thought how wrong his name was. *Amin—the trustee! Was it the trust or the breach of it? Trust, hope, struggle for a better world, are all figments of imagination, whereas the body, the senses and their comfort are a reality*. He was now following the cops to the small room where the hands of Quddoos were shackled on his back with dog chain. He was lying flat on the floor.

A black ferocious hound, sticking his long red tongue out and baring his razor-sharp teeth, growled and pounced at him time and again, and time and again its chain was being pulled away. In the adjoining cabin, Abu Hamza, who was picked up half-dead, lay utterly speechless, even when his skin was peeled off, his organs pulled, and incessant, deafening noise tore his ear drums.

Impossible to believe! Those who had blue eyes and firm lips, and were buried in heavy boots and weapons, were spitting out their entire stock of verbal abuses. Abu Hamza's ribs were clearly visible. On his chest were dark bruises and fresh red wounds. The wounds on his legs were oozing pus. Here and there, white, thread-like insects crept on his body. There were dark bulging abrasions everywhere on his strong jaws. His hairs had fallen over his eyes like tangled yarns, and his bushy beard and nails had not forgotten to grow. His fingers were swollen like sweet potatoes, and thick yellowish liquid was dripping down from them.

"O, then he is the ringleader!" The intelligence officer looked deeply at Abu Hamza.

The officer then turned to him, "Do you know him?"

"Yes, he himself told me about his plans."

Abu Hamza cleared the tousled hairs from his eyes with his swollen fingers, and stared at him. His eyes and his face did not betray any signs of grievance, or surprise or even of any hatred.

After getting all the information, the intelligence officer lodged himself on a chair in the corner. The others also sat around him. Amin was standing in the corner and Hamza was continuously looking at him. The officer's words were reaching to him in fragments.

He was telling the rest of them that it was necessary to condition the detainees before interrogating them and making them divulge the secrets, "Their human instinct is the greatest hurdle in the way. In fact the biggest trouble with man is his human feeling itself, and more so in this race. For as long as you do not make them believe that they aren't at all human beings, they won't be of any use to you. Set up a canopy tomorrow at nine in the morning, in the enclosure outside the barracks. You've yet to learn many things there."

The intelligence officer gave his instructions and went out whistling.

Subsequently, the next day, a canopy was put up not before half past nine. The entire crowd of the barracks was brought together there.

So many people! Amin was astonished. *Aren't they those who were traceless for months, those who were counted among the dead?'* He tried to look at all of them carefully.

Perhaps all this was the gathering of the dead. That was the reason why there was silence everywhere in spite of the presence of so many.

Awesome stillness pervaded in the atmosphere! Nothing besides that! And then, sounded the trumpets, followed by the bugle. With the bugle sound, the heavy iron-gate opened, and through it the spectacle, in its entirety, walked into the canopy. A uniformed woman soldier, her breasts swelling above her waist-belt, was leading it. Her brown hair was sneaking out from all sides of her military cap. She held the end of a thick chain in her hand, the other end of which was tied to the neck of a moving figure.

It was not clear what that stirring being was—a man or a dog. It, nevertheless, was crawling on all fours—bulkier than a dog, stark naked. Its nakedness was as evident as that of the other animals. And its bony skeleton was moving on all fours. Its mouth was lifted up like the snout of an animal, and his scraggly beard was dripping.

Do dogs have beard? He asked in his head.

The woman soldier kept on violently jerking the chain in her hand, and the *four-footed* figure's neck would turn on every jerk. She would then blow a vigorous kick with her heavy heeled military boot on its rear. And throwing glances over to the crowd with a triumphant look, she would wave her other free hand.

The intelligence officer now came out of a row of officers standing at the centre of the canopy. He gestured towards the woman soldier making a sign of V with his two fingers, and cried, "Bravo, keep it going!"

Hearing words of encouragement, the woman became more alert. The intelligence officer looked up boastfully, and gestured to the skeletal figure that had a chain round its neck.

He kicked on its snout with his heavy boots and called out: "Dog . . . dog . . . bow . . . wow . . ."

Half of the crowd laughed loudly. The other half remained silent. The officer then, signaled in a direction, and many photographers came running, laden with every kind of cameras. Then, two soldiers came in the middle of the field, zipped open their flies, and started emptying their urine on the *four-footed* figure. It gagged under the stinking yellow liquid, fretted on all fours to protect its head, mouth and eyes.

"Oh, ho!" the woman soldier pulled the chain. It was strange that the woman had such enormous force and strength. Abu Hamza collapsed on all fours. His throat emitted a sickening, non-human sound. And the cameras went on clicking faster and faster . . . click . . . . click.

Meanwhile, the trumpets again sounded. The crowd was now dispersing. In a little while, the soldiers vanished into their barracks, except the woman soldier and her captive. In that now deserted, black canopy, the *four-footed* figure was still lying on the ground, and the woman soldier was still jerking his collar belt, and at every jerk a non-human sound broke out of his throat, breaking the deathly silence ruling the place.

14. THE BONSAI

Asif Farrukhi

It is growing colder as the night is wearing on. Defying the shivering chill, I am standing in the atrium, tending my plants. The beauty and brilliance of the flowering plants is unfolding the secret behind my standing up to the freezing weather. The fruit of my defiance is sprouting from their stems, their boughs, their thorns, and their every leaf. Their splendor is manifest to all. Perhaps, I alone have missed to observe it.

I have been all too busy waxing the colours of the leaves throughout the night. But before I could realize it, one of the plants in the room, has started to die, leaf by leaf. I sit there right in front of that plant, pressing my one hand against my heart, while the other keeps inadvertently running, shining the leaves, even though they have already turned lush green.

Looking at the brilliant colour of the spotless new leaves, who can say for how long they have been rubbed and wiped clean? It is one of the many plant pots adorning the small greenhouse in my new house. The first ray of daybreak crosses like an arrow through the window-panes, and the leaves brighten up one by one.

Those who enjoy the blooming green leaves in the yellow sun, and stop to have a look at them, may never know how hard I have striven to keep them like that. For as long as the sunlight stays, my eyes keep watching their verdant colour without a wink.

As night arrives, I get on my job—watering the plants, turning the soil, digging it up and mixing plant food in it. I take great care in following word by word, the directions written on the fertilizer box. I get these boxes imported to me, and always ask my travelling friends to bring me the same plant food and plant medicine, in the hope that if they suit my plants, my effort to fertilize the soil to make them grow and come into blossom, will be rewarded.

After cleaning the rims of the flower pots, I reach to the leaves; bathe them with water, washing out their nocturnal indolence and diurnal dust. I spray them when they are washed fresh. I order the specific brand of spray from abroad, especially because that company guarantees its use will not block the pores, and so the natural texture of the leaves can never be destroyed. The spurious products stuffing the markets these days are, otherwise, not to be trusted. After spraying the leaves, I take particular care to wipe them softly with tissue papers.

I clean the leaves by puffing out wisps of steam, and then each leaf starts sparkling like glass. Their lush green colour appears to brighten me too. I water these plants, and exist with them as they liven up. But I haven't disclosed my feelings to anybody. My wife often comes in and stands beside me, when I water them late at night, and clean their leaves. When she finds me busy with my plants, she returns to her room disappointed, saying nothing.

After I finish my job, I collect my sprayer, plant trimmer, and the tissue paper box, switch off the lights, and throwing a look on the plants move out, leaving them to darkness and to sleep. After a little while, the fading darkness of dawn thickens in the room, and the coconut rind, bound to keep the plants soft, starts drying out.

I can still clearly recall, lying in bed in the stillness of night, the day when my wife approached me with a small new flower pot in her hands. I couldn't immediately foresee whether that unexpected gesture of hers was a sort of forewarning.

"Look what I've brought for you!" She held the pot before me, smiling.

I looked at her face before surveying the pot and the plant in it. Her eyes were also smiling, and fine wrinkles had started to appear round their corners. Crow's feet, I knew them by their name. But it didn't cross my mind then. I was thinking of something else. Why was that strange smile playing on her face? Was it the happiness of getting me a gift I really liked, or a supercilious sneer?—A smile that seems like snubbing me, saying *'Look how much I care for you while you ignore me and give all your care to your plants!* Her arrogance became more obvious when I accepted the plant, and put it with the others, in the centre of the glasshouse. Her smile caused me no fear or anxiety. I was just overtaken by surprise.

"Is it really for me?" I asked to affirm.

"Oh yes! Why not?" She replied sharply.

"But how could you finally find anything for me? You've always been saying you can't decide what to bring for me." I tried my best to keep my voice steady.

"Oh dear! You turn into a cactus on petty matters. Aren't you pleased to see what I've brought for you?"

I had noticed the rise and fall in her voice. Had I not listened to her then, the footfall of the storm would have grown louder.

So, I looked up at her. *What's this? Why are you talking like that?* But I didn't ask her any of these questions that beset me then. She, somehow read them on my face.

"You flaunt a great fondness for flowers, don't you? And yet you can't tell this plant. This is a *Bonsai*! Have you seen one like this, ever?" Her tone betrayed a strain of victory—the victory of taking me by surprise.

"I was passing through the market, when I saw this in the glass window of a shop. My mind immediately turned towards you. I thought I must get it! Oh, no, no! I'm wrong. It wasn't this plant. I saw something else in the showcase. It was a new perfume that I wanted to buy for myself. But I didn't. This plant was displayed on one of those trolleys that people set up on the ground floor of shopping malls, on weekends. The vendor had many other plants on his cart. This *Bonsai* pot sat there alone among other different plants, of which you already have a lot. I felt instantly that you would appreciate this plant, which is not there in your collection. Do you know what a *Bonsai* is?"

I was waiting for her to stop. Obviously, I knew about the *Bonsai* plants. It was another matter that I hadn't thought of owning one, though. I felt it was something to be seen from a distance; something that looked nice in display only. I knew well enough that it needed great care and attention. Who, after all, would like to invite that trouble?

But now that she had brought it, I had to accept it with both my hands. As if this was not enough, I had to say some proper words of thanks, and put across a few formal expressions of my happiness or surprise at getting the gift. I felt I must as a mark of courtesy, and of encouragement, thank her for such a sweet gesture.

My thoughts were broken by her nonstop monologue, "Oh sorry, I clean forgot that it was you who introduced me first to the *Bonsai* plant and its specific features. Wasn't it you who had told me earlier, that a *Bonsai* has to be regularly cultivated, and also that the plant has something like, what you said, a metaphysical significance?"

"Yes, they grow up with great difficulty," I said just for the sake of it, and taking the *Bonsai* pot, went where other plants were waiting for me and the night.

The night's darkness had eclipsed the house, filling it with its own voices and shadows. I got up in the midst of these voices, and found my way to the greenhouse. There seemed to be something new about the darkness there. Lights, on the contrary, are all alike and unexciting. I prepared myself to grope around in the gathering darkness. Since the day I entered this house, I had been walking into the deepening gloom, every night, all the way to my plants, hearing them breathe like living beings, in the lengthening shadows of the night,.

They feel chlorophyll molding in their bodies, converting sunlight into food and energy, nourishing their leaves with luxuriant greenness, and their branches with pulp. The darkness in the house consumes these plants. I always find myself panic stricken, when my eyes suddenly open in the middle of the night. *Where am I? How the hell have I come here? What is going to happen now*?

Whenever fear overtakes me, I try to think about my plants. I close my eyes and feel my body stiffening in the mossy darkness, the skin baking dry and rough, the green fluid running in my arms, and chlorophyll rolling down, covering my arms with leaves, so in a short while my arms get covered with leaves. My legs automatically slip into the slippers without creating any sound.

Following my instincts, I open the door, come out, leaving the door on latch, and climb the stairs, counting the steps at guess. I know where to take a turn, without banging against the wall, and where to stop in order to reach near the plants.

My waking up and getting out for the plants, coincides with the time when the sun goes to sleep in the windows of the house. The distant sky is visible from the windows of the other houses—a blackish sky, moving away, withdrawing. The place where I usually go first, and stay for long is under a skylight. From its four equilateral glasses, the sky appears to be sloping, shaking feverishly, and stooping down, as if in a few moments, the roof will open like a lid, leaving us exposed under the dark open sky.

The loftiness of the sky is clearly evident from there. Dense, dark clouds, with their wings fastened to one another, keep on flying over the skylight, and I watch their moving, shaking shadows sifting through the glasses. The shadows spread on the floor, and walking on them I enter the glasshouse, which is filled with the thick, gathering rows of plants. The rows of plants are kept in a neat sequence. The bowl-shaped flower pots, with round glazed chip work, are perched on the stand, from whose soil, creepers sprout forth, and cover a good part of the floor.

Sometimes, when I accidently step on their feathery leaves, they remind me of those girls who, in ancient times, used to welcome their *Peshwas*[1] by spreading their long, dark tresses on the way. Even at night my bare feet recognizes that touch. In fact the pots contain those indoor plants that I have collected in years. I tell myself that they can only grow in the open area, as if presenting a justification for shifting them to that quiet, isolated corner of the town, where I have built my new house. As the plants mature, blossom and flourish, I also grow with them. I spend the murky darkness of the night trimming them, watering them, and loosening their soil. The light slipping through the skylight is enough for me.

But that night my steps faltered. Perhaps, the *Bonsai* had crept into my mind in the midst of other plants. It must surely be there sitting between the others. As I was thinking about it, a voice overwhelmed me. Rustling noises gushed forth from all directions. It appeared as if the sky had fallen down and people were wailing loudly, or screaming airplanes were passing from over the skylight. I was struck with consternation for a moment. What plants, what luxuriance! This deafening noise had removed everything from my mind. I then realized that I had overstepped the security alarm border line, letting the it screech.

My wife had so many times explained to me that there was a seeing eye in the alarm system, beyond the wall. The alarm though expensive, was necessary for us. It was a must for those living in the Defence Society area. The housing colony was expanding, and as the residential quarters proceeded towards the Creek, which was going to be filled any day now, causing escalation in the cost of residential lands, the need for security was also growing.

My wife herself had selected the security company from among many others in the newspaper advertisements that she had rummaged through. She had the security system installed in the indoor area of the house during the finishing stages of its construction.

The red security light flickered off and on, like a staring eye. It was not only giving a fixed flash. It was moving in all directions, indicating the place from where security lapses were taking place. Either the door on the first or the window on the ground floor was open.

My wife always switched off the lights at night before sleeping, with the same punctuality and care, with which our grandmother, in our childhood days, enclosed us in safety after reciting "*Ayat-al-Kursi*[2] and clapping thrice.

"There are blessings in abundance in these *Holy Verses*, my son." She used to say when she saw me laughing at her claps. She would then narrate the story, "They protect people from dangers. There was an old woman who didn't completely remember these *Holy Verses*. When she left her house she recited instead,

'Ayat-al-Kursi
Wake, wake everybody
Thieves are coming, see!
Turn them blind ye',

A thief once entered the house, and by the Will of God, he turned into a . . ."

But the echo of grandma's voice broke like the reel of an old film, subdued by another voice. It was my wife's who was standing in front.

"You've again stepped in front of that light, haven't you?"

She asked me irritably, "How many times have I arranged demonstrations for you? But you're rarely in your senses. You must have sat among your plants again. You and your plants! Now, don't keep standing there, looking at my face like that. Go, switch off the alarm! Or else, its shriek will deprive me of any rest and sleep."

I walked, as if in sleep, towards the alarm, which was screeching like a wailing ambulance steering through the fast-flowing traffic on the town streets. The shrieking ambulance always worried me, pushing me to think if the life inside it was going to be saved, or wiped out.

But my wife's shriek didn't portend any loss of life. It heralded, however, the loss of identity, my own identity. I moved safely maneuvering through my plants, extended my hand and fed the number, which was the first part of the alarm code. The alarm turned off. Nobody said anything. For a heavy moment, stony silence hung over the room. It was again broken by a sound. It was the telephone now.

"It must be the security personnel checking the alarm. Pick up the phone. Quick!" She ordered.

I walked ahead in obedience. The voice on telephone sounded peevish and insipid, as if deprived of a sound sleep.

The security staff at the other end of the phone spoke in our agreed sign language with words from the natural world of vegetation, and disconnected the phone on getting a satisfactory reply. I felt that they might have been laughing at my giving a false alarm once again. People are not always considerate when you embarrass them over and over again. The words of the code again kindled my concern for the plants, making me restless to go near them.

To me the most surprising thing about the *Bonsai* was that it was, after all, a plant. Planted in an ordinary small clay pot, irrespective of its size, it was complete in itself. There was no imperfection in it—nothing that might have stunted its growth, or broken it, or was cut out of it. I took the pot in my hands, turned it round before my eyes, and observed it intently. Two branches sprouted from a dried stalk. This was its trunk. Young leaves were shooting out from its branches. They were tiny leaves, soft like a newborn baby's fingers, squeezed in its closed fists, yet complete in them. I continued watching it. It was a real pine tree.

I had always remembered the term *Bonsai* with the sense impression of juniper forests on lofty mountains and in valleys. The mere thought of it filled the fragrance of forests in my mind. I had never ever imagined that I could stand in the room, holding in a mere flower pot, the fragrance wafting along by the breeze. My instant reaction was to put it back in its place. You cannot seize fragrance. You should never even try doing it. But I did what I felt was the smallest gesture of civility. I held the *Bonsai* pot in my hands for quite some time, because I remembered who had given me that.

She had told me that that was a gift from her. A certain king of the ancient times too had sent gifts of gouged eyes, packed in a case to someone, I knew not who.

"You're wrong to think that this pruning into a *Bonsai* causes pain to the tree." Her voice was clear and curt. It cut through the reigning silence, like scissors, and shone like a blade in the darkness. "I checked on the internet about *Bonsais*. They are prepared by a very special procedure which is called styling. It is the law of grow and clip in which all unnecessary parts of a tree are pruned."

Our characters had changed. Today she was bent upon teaching me, "It's for this very reason that people call it a living statue. The tree has been given this shape through wiring."

I looked back. She was gone, leaving the place to murky darkness and to me.

A shadow formed on the floor, under the dim skylight. It was a broken, incomplete shadow—the shadow of a branch with thorns. I couldn't dare to look at it continuously. All my plants stood silent, bowing their heads. They appeared to me like those grimy, untidy children of the village school, who felt ashamed to come before the fresh and tidy boys of the wealthy household. Their leaves were soiled, and their colours paled.

The night was departing, and the leaves were not yet cleaned. I again picked up the *Bonsai* pot sitting among the other plants. Its branches were thin and delicate, and its leaves sparse. It had a finished design, though. Completely perfect! Like the moulded porcelain figure. Like a toy. Like the dwarf who couldn't reach his completion. It was weeping in the pot, nay crying, as if to make me hear it. Its piteous lament was so loud that I could see it in the contours of its leaves and twigs.

The sound of its cry was like the soft shrill whistle of a bird. It was sniveling, twirling, stamping its feet, struggling hard, restlessly trying to come out of the pot. It wanted to free itself from the wire that had tangled it; to straighten its bowing boughs, join the severed branches. It craved to grow, to expand.

Fearing that the pot might slip from my hands, like persistently stubborn children breaking away from the clutches of their mother, I put it on the floor before it slipped and broke into pieces.

It was absolutely silent now. There was no sound, no shadow. Its boughs and the needles sprouting from them, if you can call them so, were all quiet. They didn't even have the motion that normally trees have, when the wind blows. Nothing was shaking, not even a rustle could be heard.

I could have endured had it cried. But its silence ran me down. I might have collapsed there. It was inviting everybody to watch it.

It was then that I understood what it signified. I stood motionless, bending my knees and holding my hands together tightly, pressing them inside. I must occupy the least space, and get my unnecessary parts trimmed.

It looked like centuries had passed, when I suddenly heard a footfall there.

"You're still there? What have you been doing standing like that?" There was anger in her tone.

It was now impossible for me to hide the truth from her.

"I'm transformed into a *Bonsai*! But please don't undo my wires. I'm still sprouting. Leave me to myself till I grow. I haven't yet ripened," I said to her, and stood stock-still in my place.

For me, now any possibility of moving away from there was automatically eliminated.

15. THE STRONG TETHER-PIN

Abdus Samad

Stepping out of the airplane, I didn't even faintly imagine my maternal uncle, Junaid, too would take the trouble of coming to the airport to receive me. When I reached the lobby, his coloured, waving handkerchief glistened before my eyes. He was standing right there in the balcony with my cousin Nissar, my *Barey Abba's*[1] son. Oh, no he wasn't just standing there. He was dancing with delight. The fountain that had dried since long, burst out from my eyes on receiving so much affection from him.

He held me in a passionate embrace, for quite some time. All the while, Nissar had been craving to even touch me, and was held from doing so by Uncle

Junaid's wrapping embrace. It was only when Uncle Junaid freed me from his embrace and his volley of questions that I could see him properly.

Uncle Junaid insisted me to stay with him. He said he would not mind if go just to meet Barey Abba, my paternal uncle, whenever I wished. The man didn't hesitate to remind me that staying with Barey Abba would not be comfortable for me. I, however, was not ready to accept that. I had traveled such a long distance only to meet my paternal uncle whom we had been calling Barey Abba since our childhood.

Uncle Junaid's picture didn't even faintly appear in my mind. I was surprised at his irrelevant insistence. But since he had come all the way to receive me at the airport, I could only refuse his offer with polite entreaties, not before promising to breakfast with him at his house, the next morning.

So I went with Nissar. Barey Abba, who had grown considerably old and couldn't rush forth to greet me, he couldn't even stand easily. But his liquid, tear-filled eyes and lined and angelic face exuded so much love and affection that I could not control myself. I rushed to him and buried my head in his lap. His trembling hands felt my head and stroked it gently. Tears welled up in his eyes, and the warm drops fell on my brow. Those drops carried many stories in them, apart from their warmth.

I lifted my head after a long while and answered all his caring queries. Looking around, I found that plight and decay were evident from every nook and cranny of the house. Though the glimpses of past grandeur manifested themselves here and there, it needed a discerning eye to discover them.

A considerable portion of the mansion lay in ruins; the rest had begun to crumble. The only liveable place was a spacious hall, and a room adjoining it, which was perhaps Barey Abba and *Bari Amma's*[2] bedroom. They spent their daytime in the hall, offering prayers and meeting people. A worn Persian carpet covered a good part of the floor in the hall. The patterns and designs on the carpet had faded away, horribly exposing its rough surface with all its clumsiness.

Two chandeliers hung from the roof of the hall. Most of their cut-glass lamps were broken; the remaining ones were covered in thick layers of dust. I had seen chandeliers like these at the museum in Belgium. Outside, on either side of the broken stairs, sat two big spouted earthen jugs. The intricate carvings on them were swathed in soot and grime. The chandeliers and the jars, all had lost their past splendour, but they bore silent testimonies to my uncle's past—a past that could not be separated from the present, and which was its strongest bond.

Barey Abba had arranged his own bedroom for me, and had moved his bed to a corner of the hall. I strongly refused to accept this hospitality. He laced his offer with numerous justifications to convince me, all of which I rejected one by one, and finally laid my bed in the hall.

During all this Uncle Junaid didn't cross my mind even once. I recalled him suddenly, after I had a lengthy earnest talk with Barey Abba and Bari Amma. I informed them that I intended to go to Uncle Junaid's for breakfast the next morning.

"Oh, Junaid! Where did you meet him?" Barey Abba stared at me for an answer.

My face bore no expression, and I replied plainly, "He came to receive me at the airport"

"Really?" He gave me a meaningful smile. My cousin Nissar hadn't perhaps told him about our meeting.

"You know Barey Abba, I was very happy to find Uncle Junaid showering so much affection on me. We must be thankful to God for having such a man around us in our family."

Barey Abba became silent, but a mysterious smile kept sticking to his lips, enhancing its meaningfulness.

Uncle Junaid's house was a feast to the eyes. It was no less than a palace in that small town. He had spent a lot on its construction, as well as on its decoration. Every room had a different colour, with matching curtains, and each was individually furnished with antique furniture.

My astonishment overtook me, and Uncle Junaid stirred it further, "You know, every room here is decorated after the guest rooms at the *Oberoi Palace Hotel* in *Srinagar*[3]."

I had never visited Srinagar, though the *Oberoi Palace* there was not unknown to me. Once it had been the palace of the Raja of Kashmir. I couldn't help feeling impressed by Uncle Junaid's keen eye for antiquities.

He took great interest in showing me every little thing in his house. Sure enough, he had collected them with great diligence. He bought any novelty that he found being sold at a cut price by the once wealthy noblemen. If he found a once upon a time rich man in dire need of money, he helped him by buying his priceless possession. If he saw any rare object at a lumber-dealer, he immediately bought it at his asking price. And he always requested his globe-trotting friends to bring him rare things from abroad.

I saw some very ordinary things in his house on which he had put the label of an original designer object with such dexterity that no one could tell. In fact, he had found out a profession for himself that spurred on his passion for collecting unique things.

As a matter of fact he did every kind of work that he could lay his hands on, but his main job was to buy at a throw away price, the farms, orchids, houses and the priceless antiques owned by ruined and needy gentle, old men of the nobility, and sell them to rich, raffish showmen at a very high price. If any of those things kindled his curious eyes, he would just keep them for himself.

Most of the handles and hinges on the doors and wardrobes in the house were antiques. The abundance of these valuable objects from the ancient past had made his house more interesting. With the arrival of wealth, he had also developed a fondness for throwing parties every now and then.

Among his guests were those magistrates, politicians, and newly rich people of his district with whom he had close contacts. He took great care to invite those old and rich noblemen as well, whose fame, pomp and glitter had not yet faded. The guests spent much of their time watching Uncle Junaid's fascinating collections with awe and interest.

The dining table had a revolving and shining glass top. The excellent, exotic and elaborate dishes that adorned Uncle Junaid's dining table were culinary delicacies that needed a lot of time and effort to prepare—something very rarely seen in our jet age.

Who after all had the patience and time needed to prepare such lavish cuisine?

"Uncle, is this a breakfast or a heavy dinner? Even as dinner, it could run for many days," I spoke, looking at the dining table.

Uncle Junaid's eyes sparkled with delight. The arrow that I had unwittingly shot, had perhaps hit the target. He replied in a voice inebriated with self-pride, "Oh no, my dear nephew! I've laid for you all that's needed for a breakfast. It's just the beginning of the receptions on your visit."

"Really uncle, we can't finish all in just one sitting," I replied with utter humility.

It was my maternal aunt's turn now, "Come on my son! No one expects the guests to eat all that's there on the table. You can eat whatever you like . . ."

"But I'm not a guest, aunt!" I put in humbly.

"You're the most important guest. You've travelled thousands of miles to visit us. Do you remember how many years you've taken to visit us?"

Uncle Junaid was, however, all hospitality. I didn't consider it proper to stretch the talk too far, and started tasting the dishes. They were so many that it would have taken a long time even calling them by name. In fact, I couldn't identify many of them. I had forgotten the tastes of a good number of dishes, because their preparation needed so much time and labour that they had become automatically obsolete for me.

But the mysterious and hidden layers of the tongue have such sensitive taste buds that they refresh even the long forgotten tastes. There were many varieties of fish cutlets. The fillets were wrapped with the gram-flour powder and spices, and fried till crispy on the outside. Their taste and their appearance tingled my memory.

I had not yet forgotten the tastes of cutlets I ate at my own home. I couldn't, for obvious reasons, deem it proper to request for them at Barey Abba's house. Finding cutlets with almost familiar taste at Uncle Junaid's, I relished them to my heart's contentment. I tasted other dishes too, and enjoyed them all a great deal.

After breakfast, Uncle Junaid provided a detailed and graphic account of all his rare collections. I had just a few days with me, and I wanted to spend most of them with Barey Abba, because I wasn't sure when again I could be able to see him. But the extraordinarily tasty dishes I had eaten at Uncle Junaid's were fomenting in my stomach a strong sense of loyalty to the provider of those dishes. My mind and tongue were under the tutelage of my tummy.

Most of the curios in Uncle Junaid's treasure trove were rare and antiquated. There were silver vessels, engraved betel-boxes, hookahs, gaudy, glittering cloaks, swords of silver, and splendidly embellished sheaths, expensive, gold picture frames and so on . . . .

Perhaps Uncle Junaid had not paid any attention to modern artefacts. I was lost for quite long in the dazzle of the antiques and became oblivious of the present. It was almost lunch time, when I returned to my senses and asked his leave.

He looked at me with surprise and asked, "Come on, who is going to dine with us?"

"Very sorry, uncle! But I have promised Barey Abba to have lunch with him today. He may mind it if I'm not there," I offered an excuse.

He laughed wryly, "Oh, you're too innocent, my dear nephew! I know he would never do so. After all, you haven't come to strangers. This is your house as well. In fact, he'll be very happy to know you have lunched with me."

I hesitated for a while, and finally told him my mind, "But I've taken my leave of him for only some time. Besides, I've had a very heavy breakfast. Honestly uncle, I've no appetite for lunch. Even with Barey Abba, I'll just keep his company at the dining table."

Uncle Junaid was not in a mood to let me off so easily, "Young man, won't it dishearten your aunt? She had been up in the kitchen since morning, preparing food for you. Just taste it if you can't eat much."

I didn't wish to disappoint Barey Abba, so the chain of hospitality with which Uncle Junaid had bound me, had to snap.

I got up with a jerk, saying, "Uncle, please forgive me for today. I'll come and dine with you some other day. Allow me to leave now, please!"

Uncle Junaid very reluctantly allowed me to go, but on the condition that I must revisit him soon.

I almost ran out to the street to Barey Abba's house which was not far. My conscience was pricking me. Entangled in the pleasures of the senses at Uncle Junaid's house, I had wasted the precious time that I had so carefully saved to stay with Barey Abba. I had never thought my plan would be disrupted just for the sake of whetting my appetite.

My apprehension proved me true.

Barey Abba was sleeping, having waited for me for too long. My head hung in shame with a terrible feeling of guilt.

Bari Amma came to my aid at that moment, and consoled me, "Don't trouble yourself so much, son. Your Barey Abba is always sleepy. Tell me, is it the time to go to sleep? He takes forty winks many times in a day."

Though she was speaking in a hushed tone, Barey Abba woke up and spoke out, "Good to see you back, my son! You've stayed out too long."

"Uncle, as a matter of fact, Uncle Junaid . . ."

I had just succeeded in recovering from the feeling of mortification, when Barey Abba sat up in his bed and cutting me short, said with a smile, "I can well imagine, my son, Junaid must have spread a very elaborate dinner table for you. And his talks! He might have just started talking when you left him."

"Exactly, that was the real problem Barey Abba. I entreated him so many times but he allowed me to leave only after I took your name."

I was relieved that Barey Abba didn't take any serious note of my long absence. On the contrary, he appeared to enjoy hearing how I spent my time there.

He asked me curiously, "What blessings lay waiting for you on Junaid's dinner table?"

I was dying to give the details, but held my tongue. Something inside stopped me from doing so. There was no need to explain all that to Barey Abba.

I just gave a vague reply, "Oh, nothing special! It was all what they eat normally everyday."

"Come on my son, surely Junaid didn't invite you with so much affection and fervour on a simple, everyday breakfast," Barey Abba was now in a mood to know the details.

Finding no escape route, I surrendered, "Yes, Barey Abba, the dishes were many and savoury. But what I liked most were the fish cutlets. I was having them after a very long gap. But there was nothing else that was so special, except, of course, that there were plenty of dishes."

"And what about his rare collections? Didn't you see them?" Barey Abba appeared to know everything about Uncle Junaid.

"Of course I did. He has turned his house into an interesting museum. I was surprised to see the priceless antiques that he has collected. In truth, Uncle Junaid seems to be very fond of putting his possessions on display."

Barey Abba gave a loud laughter, though a nasty bout of coughs swooped on it. He took it long and hard to get a release from it. All that while my aunt rubbed his back gently, and I too gave her a helping hand.

He recovered after some time and continued the discussion between short deep breaths, "Yes, your last sentence is quite correct. He has a strong tendency for openly flaunting his wealth. He has taken pains to collect so many things for this very reason. I don't know whether he told you that they were his ancestral possessions."

"I didn't understand you uncle!" I enquired politely.

"He always tells people in graphic details about the ancestry of each of his possessions which as he said belonged to his such or such ancestors . . . ," Barey Abba's face creased into a smile.

"Isn't that true?" I cut him short.

He smiled again and asked, "Don't you really know some basic facts about your Uncle Junaid?"

"I couldn't really get you, uncle."

I didn't, till that moment, had any doubts regarding the facts about the legitimacy of Junaid Uncle's claims.

Barey Abba was going to say something when Bari Amma interrupted, "Leave it! What's the use of all that gossip now? How is talking about Junaid really going to help you? Just leave him as he is. Pray to God that everyone else's life also changes for the better."

Barey Abba fell quiet for some time. I waited for him to say something. He finally spoke in muted voice, "Children, after all, must know something about their family."

"Where's the need for it? However indirectly, eventually he belongs to our family. The world knows it well. You'll only waste your time exposing the facts about him. Get ready, I am going to lay the table," Bari Amma's wisdom was laying itself bare.

It looked as if she was the lighthouse that had lighted the hearts and minds of experienced, forbearing, and wise people like Barey Abba. They were married for over fifty years. And during these years she appeared to have illuminated all corners of his mind and life with the light of her sagacity and wisdom. She was the woman who had taken him out from the blazing furnace of family wrangles and transformed him into pure gold. Though I hadn't seen him fifty years back, but I could see that in her prudence and sagacity.

Bari Amma spread dinner on the wooden bed in the hall. I didn't feel it nice sitting there, being entertained like a guest, when I saw her bringing the dishes and plates from the kitchen. So, I got up and in spite of her insistence, helped her lay the table. She had prepared a very special dinner. Fried potato slices with spices, lady's finger with boiled eggs, steamed lentil, stewed mince balls . . .

When Barey Abba washed his hands and sat for dinner, I took a look at all the dishes and uttered, "Why am I taken as a guest here, Barey Abba? Is there any need for these formalities? I'd have loved to eat what you eat everyday in the house."

He glanced up at me, drawing a long breath. I quickly realized I should not have said this to him.

He remarked, after a little pause, "There was a time when we ate simple dishes like these as a change from the daily consumption of rich food. The time has come now that today we are entertaining our son, who has travelled long distances to see us, with the same dishes. There are no formalities for you, my son."

"I am awfully sorry, Barey Abba. I just spoke absently. What to talk of eating these dishes, I've been waiting since long to relish them."

I tried to eat with utmost delight, although the food I savoured at Uncle Junaid's house was still rumbling in the stomach. There was no room left for more. Nevertheless, the empathy, the long lost aroma, exuding from the food my aunt had prepared for me, called for justice, even in the face of impossibility. I, therefore, sat down with all my heart and soul to be as fair as I could be to the food.

After the meal, I lay down on the wooden bed. Barey Abba was in a talkative mood, and he talked at length about our family history. He related how our family suffered, what caused its financial breakdown, who was responsible for it, what actions or inactions expedited it, and how the large and bold writings on the wall were completely overlooked.

Nowhere in his entire narration was there anything particular that could have surprised me. During the partition of India millions of families suffered the same fate, and had the same stories to tell. Whenever the nobility in this country inherited or seized power and wealth, it did nothing but spent a life of sheer luxury and indulgence. It wasted all its money on inventing amazing varieties of elaborate and delicious dishes, and on exploring other worldly pleasures.

I was not at all interested in such stories. I had heard and read a lot about incidents that had wrecked families in our part of the world. I kept on expressing an *aye* each time that Barey Abba paused for a breath. Though I was feeling very sleepy, I stayed awake only for his sake.

When he finished venting his spleen, a long held question escaped my tongue, "So how are things going on in this house, Barey Abba?"

I knew if anyone else had asked the same question how angry he would have become. But I was the son of the family. I had a right to know that. He grew silent and his face took on a thoughtful expression. I held my breath for as long as he was quiet. I was worried lest he might take it as an affront. God forbid if he really did, in which case my visit would have gone to waste. It was only for his pleasure that I had come to see him.

Barey Abba started despondently, "What is left there to say, my son? We have no means left for a regular income. The compensation bonds granted in lieu of the confiscation of our estates by the government had long since exhausted. Farms and orchards have all been sold out, bit by bit. We tried to get your cousin Nissar some education, but he was also overtaken by bad luck. He works as a clerk in a provision shop and supports himself. As for us, it is this ruin that is only left to see us through the remaining days of our lives. I get some loans on this property, and that is all."

I was not satisfied with Barey Abba's answer, but I didn't dare to request him for more details. So, I considered it proper to go to sleep.

Bari Amma woke me up the next morning and announced, "Junaid has sent his servant for you. Have you promised him to be there today?"

"Uncle Junaid's servant? Promise?" I could not understand anything. However, I got up, and after changing my dress went out to see. The man was waiting for me.

"Sir, the master is waiting for you at the breakfast table," the servant informed me with great respect.

I replied in a slightly dismissive tone, "Oh, no! How can I come now? I can't come before . . ."

There was no point in going again to breakfast at Uncle Junaid's house, and that too in a sudden rush. My sole intention to visit the place was to stay with Barey Abba. I preferred to eat simple food with him than dine out on savoury meals.

I tried to control myself and told Uncle Junaid's servant, "Please ask Uncle Junaid to take his breakfast, I could be able to visit him only after a few hours," and returned inside without waiting for an answer.

Bari Amma had cooked fried bread, fried potato slices with turmeric, and green coriander chutney. My taste buds recognized the flavours they had relished long time back.

Barey Abba was picking up tiny morsels in a slow motion. With his head bowed, he asked me, "Had Junaid invited you today also?"

I stayed my hand, and staring at him replied in a rising tone, "There was nothing like that, Barey Abba. He just asked me to dine with him again any day I liked. It doesn't mean that I keep on going to him everyday. I haven't come here to accept generous hospitalities. I've come to my house, to you and my Bari Amma. And that's that."

I saw my answer brightening the dimmed eyes of Barey Abba and aunt.

He calmed me with a smile, "Junaid is no stranger to us, my son. He is in our family. You aren't a guest there. Don't break his heart, if he's showering affections on you."

I ate silently.

We sat together for quite long after tea. Barey Abba had a lot to talk about, and the more he expended it, the more he appeared to have in store. I wouldn't have cared had anyone else possessed his traits. But Barey Abba's treasure house of talks possessed those valuable gems, which dazzled my eyes. And along with my eyes, my heart and mind, and all those layers of my consciousness which the alien soil had covered with its money and expediency, brightened up with his discourse.

Among those precious gems were my deceased parents, whom I had left alive and happy. Leaving them back in India, I had travelled abroad in search of things I wasn't fully aware of. I spent many years searching for them but my hands were still empty. I had even lost what I had back home.

There were my other uncles and aunts, and scores of other relatives with whom I spent my childhood dandling in their arms, persistently imploring them to get things for me. In Barey Abba's treasure house were also stories about my grandparents, whom I had not seen, but whose memory stimulates me even today.

We didn't notice how time flew past us.

We were tolled back to the present when Bari Amma, perhaps in my sympathy, cut Barey Abba short, "How long would you go on talking. The poor boy must have become tired. Take a breath, I'm bringing tea."

"Oh, no Bari Amma, I'm not at all weary. When Barey Abba speaks, his voice possesses my body and soul. Please don't stop him," I nearly cried out.

Barey Abba, who was a little embarrassed by aunt's interference, appeared suddenly enlivened.

His face reddened with pleasure and he spoke out in excitement, "Where will he get anyone who could talk like me? We have now only memories left with us to rekindle and recite. May God help us!"

When Bari Amma brought us tea, Barey Abba's seemingly unending discourse broke as it did.

But he suddenly spoke out as if remembering something, and advised me, "Son, it's better if you go and visit Junaid. He must be waiting. He has been sending his servant for you since morning."

In truth, I didn't feel, even a little inclined to go to Uncle Junaid. I was absolutely fed up with his stereotype talks. I had already seen and understood a great deal of the world at my age. There was nothing new for me in Uncle Junaid's nattering about his opulence. But I had visited my home place only to strengthen old relationships, not to destroy them. Uncle Junaid was undoubtedly a vital link in that chain. I went, therefore, straight to his house.

There was a flare of excitement in Uncle Junaid's voice on seeing me, "O my dear nephew, I've been waiting in breathless anticipation for you since morning. Look there, the breakfast table is still covered with dishes!"

I threw a cursory glance at the huge dining table which was filled to capacity. Almost all the dishes appeared to be left untouched.

"You should have taken your breakfast uncle. I'm sorry, to have made you wait unfairly," I expressed my regret.

Uncle Junaid replied smiling, "I have had some, but just tell me how much can a lone man eat."

"Uncle, I haven't come starving from abroad, and I don't have a giant's appetite," I retorted sharply.

He put his hands on my shoulder and said, "Oh, come on! Heaven forbid, that I would ever think of anything like that. You're our guest, and so your aunt has prepared a variety of savoury dishes of your choice. Eat anything you like."

I folded my hands and pleaded, "Please don't embarrass me uncle. I am not a guest. I've come to my own house, to stay for some time with my own people. Let this feeling too stay with me. I'm immensely grateful to you and aunt for your love and care. I'd have relished my hard home-baked bread more than these wonderful, exotic victuals."

"Even then, you must try and eat something. This elaborate meal has been prepared for you," my aunt insisted gently yet firmly, and I was compelled to go to the table.

No doubt, the breakfast table bore testimony to her excessive interest in my appetite. But I had eaten to my fill with Barey Abba, and there was no room left for a morsel more. Even then, I took a bite or two for her sake.

We had just settled after breakfast, when a strikingly beautiful girl entered the room, pushing a wheelchair occupied by a young man with very ordinary features, looking incapacitated in some way.

Uncle Junaid stood up on seeing them, and addressed me, "This is your cousin sister and he's her husband. You couldn't see them on your last visit. I've called them especially to meet you today."

My cousin saluted me with a graceful bend of her head, and her husband reached out for a handshake. It was a numb and frozen hand. His face was also expressionless, save a faint smile flickering across it.

For an instant, I could not understand how to express myself. What I witnessed, failed to push me to tell him even formally that I was so happy to see him. I anyhow succeeded in suppressing my inner feelings so that my face couldn't betray me, and gave full vent to the bright smile that I had been carrying carefully on my lips from America.

Uncle Junaid introduced his son-in-law with pride and joy, and in considerable detail, "Mr. Sajid is the grandson of *Khan Bahadur*[4] *Allauddin*. His father is the most prominent lawyer in town. He belongs to an old-established family, and they have very high connections. The Prime Minister had once paid a visit to their palatial house. Sajid's father is contesting in the next election, and God willing he will become a Member of the Parliament."

Uncle Junaid was continuously looking at his beautiful daughter, while introducing his son-in-law to me. Though she was smiling, I didn't take any time in trying to discover what lay behind those smiles. I had come across those mysterious yet rueful smiles many a times in my life. Anyway, it was all his personal family matter. What concerned me most at that moment was to hold on to my smile without any change in it. I really felt that I was just a guest there, and had to leave the place as quickly as I could.

Sajid uttered nothing throughout our conversation, except for the occasional *yes* and *no*. I suspected he didn't want to talk. During our talk, Uncle Junaid informed me that Sajid didn't need to take on any job because he had so much of wealth that it could comfortably look after many of his future generations, without the need to work. Usually affluent people embrace an honourable profession to while away their time. And Sajid's father had chosen the legal profession, where too he had reached the top.

Throughout their talks Uncle Junaid and his wife didn't reveal any trace of guilt for selecting an awful mismatch for their daughter. On the contrary, they appeared unusually happy.

When I asked his leave after some time, Uncle Junaid strongly urged me to stay for lunch. But overtaken by a strange passion, I dispensed with all formalities and flatly refused. Perhaps my refusal was so intense that he couldn't repeat his offer. He, nevertheless, pulled out a promise from me that I had to dine with him some other day.

I could hardly speak when I returned home in a rotten mood. Barey Abba became uneasy and asked me, "My son, is everything all right with you? Did you see anybody else at Junaid's house?"

"I'm okay uncle! No, there weren't many people there. In fact, I met just . . ." I was so distressed that I didn't want to talk any more on the topic.

Making excuse of an upset stomach when Bari Amma called me for lunch, I went to sleep, wrapping myself up in a blanket.

I slept late into the evening, and got up refreshed. Barey Abba was waiting for me on tea. With her genuine, loving care Bari Amma asked me to eat something. I apologized, promising her politely that I would eat my supper like a horse. Barey Abba watched me intently between sips of tea, and I tried my best to evade his gaze.

He asked me softly after finishing his tea, "Did you meet Junaid's son-in-law?"

I was startled. He had somehow discovered what had been vexing me since my return from Uncle Junaid's house.

"Uncle Junaid has all God's blessings, in addition to a beautiful daughter. But Barey Abba, I don't understand what forced him, in spite of all that, to marry her off to a disabled man. And he has no regrets. He looks all too happy," my tone betrayed my protest.

He gave a laugh, but quickly controlled it, and said, "Having lived in the West for so many years, I wonder whether you'll ever understand the reason behind it. It's a fact that he's an enormously wealthy man, and his wealth is increasing day in, day out. But he was missing just one thing that perhaps he found out by marrying off his daughter in that family."

Barey Abba stopped, and I couldn't decide whether he did it deliberately, or he was really tired of talking for so long. I knew he was a man who loved talking endlessly.

I waited for him to continue, but spoke out when found him silent, "What was he missing so terribly, Barey Abba?"

He didn't speak anything for some time. Perhaps, he was seriously searching for an answer, for which I was impatiently waiting.

At last, clearing his throat he broke the silence, "I wonder, my son, whether you know that Junaid has entered into our family from a relationship that can never have a social sanction. I mean to say that his mother came from a very . . ."

I was not in a mood to listen to the details, so cutting him short in the middle, I remarked, "Issues like that don't matter much anymore, Barey Abba. No one is interested in your family history, today. The fact is that Uncle Junaid has acquired everything that a successful person is expected to have achieved in these times."

Barey Abba took a deep breath and then said, "I know you couldn't fully grasp what I was talking about. Actually, people knew Junaid didn't have any strong family background. He needed a strong support, a tether-pin, allowing him to move around in the world, getting socially recognized, amassing fame and fortune through it. To achieve that goal, he sacrificed his only daughter. His next generation would be strongly tethered with a solid background—something that very few people could claim to enjoy. His grandchildren would be known as the descendants of *Khan Bahadur Alauddin*. Junaid would then acquire broad wings to help him fly across the world."

I watched Barey Abba as he stopped. Though I understood whatever he was saying, I couldn't quite gather what he wanted me to see into it. I felt deeply uneasy the following night, vexed with mysterious and unanswerable questions.

These were questions with which I was not directly concerned. I could not, nevertheless, remain unconcerned with them. They were like real slaps in the face, when I found myself unable to answer them. I had travelled across the world, offering solutions to the seemingly intractable and complicated problems besetting my establishment where I worked. I had always lived up to the expectations of people who pinned their hopes on me in critical situations. But Uncle Junaid's story had perplexed my razor sharp mind.

I spent the whole night, plunging frequently into the deep sea of confusion and chaos, trying in vain to discover any hidden pearl of meaning, wandering through the forest of absurdities, striving fruitlessly to suggest a meaningful title for the chaos and disorder that had held my thought.

Nothing worked!

Time and again Uncle Junaid's cheerful face appeared before me, and faded away. His daughter's puzzling smile, forcing itself on her lips, rose and sank like the mysterious smile of *Mona Liza*, whose labyrinth never led me to any meaning.

Uncle Junaid's invalid, wheelchair confined son-in-law often peeped through the haze of my memory. Perhaps his disability had also left him without the power of speech. Whenever he tried to speak out he stammered so severely that the words escaping his mouth flew away, like paper boats in a fast-flowing river.

It was the first time in my life that I had so completely failed in solving the tangled threads of my thoughts. The intense feeling of defeat took my sleep away, and I lay in bed changing sides, the whole long night.

I had not come home on a planned holiday. I just wanted to spend a week or two and then leave. But I got fed up in less than a week. It appeared as though Barey Abba had poured out on me, all the treasures of memory that he had kept hidden since my absence, and he had now nothing more left to say except repeating them.

When I asked his leave to prepare for my departure, he suddenly became sad. Tears filled his eyes. I tried attentively to read his mind. I was far removed from the world of emotions that provided fodder for the thoughts of simple people like Barey Abba. True, it was the remote gust of emotions that had blown me to that place, but it was after all just a gust, which faded as it came.

"My son, I know it well that you're a very busy man, and you've spared some moment out of your precious time, only for our love and affection. The festival of *Bakrid* is due a few days from now. You don't know when again you get time to visit us. I may not live to see you then. I wish you spent *Bakrid* with us," *Barey Abba's* voice grew hoarse and heavy with emotions.

I could not decide whether the tone betrayed an order or a request, but it exuded such magic effect and so much magnetic influence that it weighed heavily over my pressing official duties. I therefore postponed my departure for a few more days.

Uncle Junaid was a man of his own type. He did not have any formal knowledge of my programme, and yet he sent his servant for me early morning the next day.

The man really irritated me, and I was going to give him a sharp reply, when Barey Abba touched my shoulder and said, "No son, Junaid loves you, and you too should try to value it. Both of you are people of the new world, though he's a bit ahead of you. He also belongs to the coming world. He has shaped his future with his own hands."

"But Barey Abba, I don't have to do anything with his future. I've come to see you, and in future also I'll come only for your sake," I voiced my protest.

"Exactly so, and that's what I'm saying. God only knows, you may not find me on your next visit. Junaid and his children will still be there as your hosts." Barey Abba's words were drowned in serenity.

I was going to raise an even greater protest when he called the servant in and told him, "Go and tell your master that his nephew will visit him after breakfast and take his lunch there."

I looked at Barey Abba in confusion.

I was an unwilling visitor at Uncle Junaid's house. He had arranged an even more lavish dinner party inspired by Barey Abba's approving message about my presence there. He had invited many prominent people of the town. I was surprised at his organizing such an elaborate party at so short a notice.

His guests were a few Central Administrative Service officers, Income Tax officers, Members of the legislative assembly, and a few top police officers. I was surprised to learn that Uncle Junaid knew fully well about my job and status abroad. But he gave an ostensibly exaggerated picture of my position, and introduced me to his guests as an Advisor to the United Nations.

I tried hard to cut him short and tell them the fact. But I don't know how the expressions in his face and eyes forced me to desist from making any clarification, and I complied. The secret was then revealed to me that he actually controlled the world around him with those mysterious expressions on his face.

He was treating his guests with an excessive politeness. Was it a civilized veneer? He never forgot to repeat his special relationship with *Khan Bahadur Alauddin* during his discussions with them, and took obvious pleasure in reminding them that whenever the Prime Minister toured the town he never forgot to visit *Khan Bahadur's* Palace. His guests looked quite impressed with his talks. Though all of them were his old acquaintances, and he must have recounted the same story to them many times over, that day had a special importance for him. He was impressing on them by talking of his high connections with the '*United Nation's Advisor*'.

At the end of the party Uncle Junaid handed out expensive presents to his guests, and they were all given through my hands. I too was given a gift through the hands of the highest officer present there. His programme was well-arranged which showed that he was really a great organizer. He took care of the smallest needs of his guests. He usually threw garden parties, birthday parties, club parties, tea parties and all, every other day.

I was like a curious toy for him, whom he presented before his guests with great enthusiasm and happiness. I got bored of all that. Too much intimacy with him started breeding contempt for the civilized veneer that had masked his real self. But it was partly Barey Abba's insistence, partly the demand of the circumstances around me that I had to bear all.

What was peculiar to Uncle Junaid was that he forced himself upon people, especially upon those with whom he wanted to become close or whom he needed. He knew the tact of impressing people, and would have succeeded even faster had he appeared less boring and more convincing and meaningful in his talks.

On the eve of *Bakrid* there was a strangely touching scene at Barey Abba's house. He was not in a position to buy goats for sacrifice. I could have done that for him, but I realized it too late and wrung my hand in distress. Nobody had drawn my attention to it, and I myself completely forgot about it. This is what happens when one loses his touch with his roots. Broken free from the tether-pin, we lose our foothold, go off the track, and float helplessly in the air. We have no choice left except bowing to the inevitable.

Bari Amma opened the old trunk, and took out the torn pieces of worn out carpets and the decaying bed sheets, and spread them on the bedsteads and the low wooden beds. Small crawling creatures had eaten up their share from many places in the carpets and the bed sheets. But they could not obliterate the traces of oriental richness woven into them. The seasoned wooden chairs were rubbed clean. The lame benches were provided with legs of bricks to make them capable of holding guests. In spite of Bari Amma's repeated assertions, prohibiting me from helping her, I turned my deaf ear and worked with her.

While making those arrangements one question kept on appearing in my mind. After all who was going to visit them on *Bakrid* and why? Barey Abba hardly appeared to have any social recognition. Then, why so much of fuss . . . ?

But what I saw at the prayer site on *Bakrid* morning was really moving. It dispelled all my earlier notions about peoples and things. After the prayer everybody flocked around Barey Abba, embracing him one by one, and making a queue before him, as if the whole gathering was looking for him only.

His shoulders seemed to have numbed. He appeared weak and exhausted. But still everyone wanted to meet him, to touch him, to see him. Of course, I also saw Uncle Junaid there. People were meeting him too. But no, people were going in the opposite direction from where he was standing. It was not they, but he who was going to people drawing them towards him.

When we returned home, I saw, to my surprise, that several dishes full of sacrificial meat were adorning the table. Discovering my amazement, Bari Amma smiled and said, "What to do my son, people send us so much on special occasions like these that we distribute a big part of them among the neighbours. Who is left in this house to eat so much? Our good luck has brought you here this year."

Barey Abba drew my attention towards him and reminded me, "My son, you should now go and meet Junaid. He must be waiting anxiously for you."

With the coming of *Bakrid*, my day of departure had also arrived. I had to leave by the late evening flight, therefore, it was quite proper for me to go and wish him good bye. I wanted to come back early from there and spend the rest of my time with Barey Abba.

Uncle Junaid was waiting for me. In fact he was going to send his servant to fetch me. He embraced me with his usual warmth, and then returned to his telephone where he was calling his acquaintances, wishing them happy *Bakrid,* and inviting them on dinner. He was sad to learn that I was leaving in the evening.

He asked me to stay for a couple of days more. I apologized, presenting to him my inability to stay for even a day more, and requested him to pay a visit to America. I knew I had chosen to stay till *Bakrid* only for the sake of Barey Abba's wet eyes.

"Uncle, God has blessed you with affluence. What better use of that money other than travelling across the world, enjoying and enriching yourself with experiences."

He thought for a while, and then spoke with a meaningful smile, "You aren't wrong, but at present I'm busy with the development of some real estate projects. I'll surely travel abroad once I'm free."

On coming back to Barey Abba's house, an absolutely astonishing sight was awaiting me. His house was full of people. God knows from where a huge crowd had swelled the place.

Barey Abba didn't have means to feed them all. He was presenting them with only cardamoms and betel-nuts, and dabbing attar on them. But seemingly unending rows of visitors were eagerly shaking his hands, greeting him on the festival day, and respectfully receiving his benedictions with dabs of attar on their clothes, before leaving the place.

All of a sudden, that part of my mind which had hitherto been entangled with vague, meaningless questions suddenly illuminated. Since my visit to my home place, those unanswered, embarrassing, and vexing questions had taken my sleep away, making my nights miserable and restless.

I now knew fully well how your roots tie you to the tether-pin, leaving you to move around independently as far as it is safe for you to not to get lost in the distant darkness. What after all, sustains you is not the physical, material possession, but something much more than that, something which has more strength and permanence—the inherent, redeeming personal qualities that shower you with genuine love, respect and peace.

I thanked God, I was leaving the place now, fully satisfied, after receiving answers that I had been anxiously looking for since my arrival.

References

1. the eldest (for male). *Barey Abba* is the father's eldest brother.
2. the eldest (for female). *Bari Amma* is *Barey Abba's* wife.
3. The capital of Indian state of Kashmir
4. a title given to the Muslim nobleman during the colonial rule in India.
5. Muslim festival of 10th of Dhu-al-Hijja (12th month of the Islamic calendar) commemorating Prophet Abraham's sacrifice.

BIBLIOGRAPHICAL NOTES

Pervez Shahidi

Pervez Shahidi (1910-1968) was primarily and genuinely an exquisite poet, and a very exquisite poet. His two anthologies 'The Dance of Life' (*Raqs-e-Hayat*) and 'The Trinity of Life' (*Tathlees-e-Hayat*) present his vision of life and are evidences of his art and ideology. He experimented with many forms of poetry, like the '*rubaiyat*' (Quatrains), *nazm*, *ghazal*, and the '*ramzia*' (The epic).

Pervez was an interesting prose writer also. His letters, essays, critical wrings, prose dramas, journalistic writings, reviews, and a short story 'The Magical Parrot' (*Tilismi Tota*), all betray his serious, innovative, and creative thinking. A multifaceted personality as an artist, *Pervez* is remembered in the world of Urdu literature for his genuine love with life, his unbinding commitment to the spirit of hope, and a passionate longing for a peaceful, ideal world. He could not write much as he died at the unripe age of fifty-eight, but whatever he wrote shows his artistic genius and his individual and singular observation of life.

Akhtar Urainvi

Akhtar Urainvi (1910-1977) was one of the foremost story writers of his time. He was writing at time when the progressive writers in Urdu were penning their popular works in prose and poetry—works that were later regarded as indelible signatures in Urdu literature. A writer of mostly short stories, *Akhtar's* stories present a blend of romanticism and reality. Intensely aware of the social, cultural, and economic realities influencing man's life and thoughts, *Akhtar* also portrays very tellingly the human aspect.

Six collections of his stories have been published. They are, in the order of their years of publication, 'Foreground and Background' (*Manzar Pas Manzar*), 'Buds and Thorns' (*Kalyan aur Kantey*), '*Cement and Dynamite*', 'The Canine Teeth and the Wings of Gabriel (*Kachliyan aur Bal-e-Jibrail*)', and 'In the Realm of Dreams' (*Sapnon key Des Mein*).

Mohammed Mohsin

Mohammed Mohsin (1910-1999), who also wrote as Mohsin Azimabadi was an acclaimed professor of Psychology in India. The plot and characters in his short stories, therefore, revolve around complex psychological symptoms or problems. The warp and woof interweaving his stories consists of the conscious and unconscious ravings of the human mind. Mohsin does not write about abstract, romantic or fanciful strains that pervade the unconscious mind. His tales are deeply rooted in the Indian social fabric, its economic and social realities.

His characters face those hard and bare realities that are their destiny. And their psychological infirmities are offshoots of a life of deprivation and misery that experience has offered them. 'The Mysterious Smile' (*Anokhi Muskurahat*) and 'The Shades of Pain' (*Lazzat-e-Azaar*) are two of his best short stories. Mohsin tried his hand at writing under the influence of the Progressive Movement which inspired Urdu literature in the forties and fifties of the last century, and which shapes the backdrop and characters of his story, 'The Labourer's Son' (*Mazdoor Ka Beta*). But Mohsin's superb craft and his deep insight into life can be discovered and appreciated in the subtlety and deftness with which he raises the curtain from the hidden secrets of human nature.

Sohail Azimabadi

Sohail Azimabadi (1911-1979), a well-known name in the genre of Urdu short stories, wrote during the times when Urdu literature was flourishing under the influence of the progressive writers who centred their art on the exploration of the common man and his besetting problems in the world where capitalism was making deep inroads into human existence. His stories portray rural life with all its defining features. But *Sohail's* characters are not prototypes, and they are not guided and goaded by the writer's ideology. They are independent men and women, articulating their own actions and reactions.

His first collection of short stories comprising of 'Bonfire' (*Alao*), 'Darkness and Light' (*Andherey aur Ujaley*), 'Two Labourers' (*Do Mazdoor*), 'The Lost Gem' (*Khoya hua Lal*), contains no romanticism while presenting the despicable life of manual workers in villages. His second volume of short stories 'Old and New' (*Nai Puraney*) appeared in 944. *Sohail's* language and characterization are natural and realistic, without any artistic embellishments.

Shakila Akhtar

Shakila Akhtar (1917-1994) started writing when Urdu *afsana* (short story) was passing through a stage of evolution from its avid concern with the external affairs socio-political realities of the time to a deeper realization of the inner conflicts and sufferings through the continual vicissitudes of circumstances. Her first story 'The Blessings' (*Rahmat*) was published in the year 1936. The background of all the stories in the anthologies, 'The Mirror', (*Darpan*), 'Hide and Seek', (*Aankh Michauli*), 'The Ugly Witch', (*Daayin*), and 'Fire and Flint' (*Aag aur Pathar*) is the portrayal of the vicissitudes of our everyday life.

The massive individual sufferings experienced by *Shakila Akhtar's* do not remain private and unidentifiable. They are transformed into universal expressions of affliction and misery. She can be classified as a feminist writer who retells the sad tales of distraught women of the social class to which she belonged. Here the awesome feeling of hopelessness creeps out of its personal contours to the expansive space outside. *Shakila Akhtar's* art is avant-garde, truly in line with the upcoming writers of the time, who believed that the overly punctuated social concerns of their predecessors and their followers were rummaging Urdu *afsana* into the realms of politics and propaganda divesting it of its literary and artistic existence.

Intezar Husain

Intezar Husain, born in 1923 is one of the most powerful, prolific, and talented Urdu fiction writers from Pakistan He writes short stories and novels in Urdu, and also columns for newspapers in English. Some of his Urdu columns are archived at Urdu-Columns.com.

He has received many awards in Pakistan, India and the Middle East. *The Seventh Door* and *Leaves* are among his books translated into English. He has translated works from English to Urdu. *Intezar Husain* stories show a fear of being irrevocably estranged from his essence, a sense that there might be no creative life possible outside one's own tradition. The death one faced within the tradition became preferable to the death that resulted from abandoning it.

The author of some one hundred twenty-five Urdu short stories, all of which have appeared in Pakistani and Indian periodicals, *Husain* has also experimented with a number of other forms: novella, novel, biography, and plays for stage, radio, and television. He has also edited a number of old Urdu tales, translated Russian and American fiction, and compiled anthologies of Urdu fiction.

Qurratul Ain Haider

Qurratul Ain Haider (1926/1928-2007) is an influential Indian Urdu novelist and short story writer. One of the most outstanding literary names in Urdu literature, she is most known for her magnum opus, *Aag Ka Darya* (River of Fire), a novel first published in Urdu in 1959, from Lahore, Pakistan, that stretches from the 4th century BC to post partition of India. Recipient of Sahitya Akademi Award (1967) for her novel The Sound of Falling Leaves (*Patjhar Ki Awaz*), Soviet Land Nehru Award (1969), *Padma_Shri* by the Government of India in 1984, *Ghalib_Award* (1985), Jnanpith Award (1989) for Travellers Unto the Night (*Akhire Shab Ke Humsafar*), *Sahitya Akademi Fellowship* (1994), Bahadur Shah Zafar Award (2000) and *Padma_Bhushan* (2005), the third highest civilian honor awarded by the Government of India, she is the foremost writer of Urdu fiction in the subcontinent.

Haider is an iconoclast. Appearing after Krishan Chander, Manto, Bedi, and Chughtai, four famous names in Urdu fiction, Haider changed the temperament of Urdu fiction. She enlarged the canvass of Urdu fiction to such an enormous expanse where times, centuries, cultures, histories, and the destinies of men and women melt into one another to produce a work of art which is timeless in scope. Her stories and novels have been translated into many languages.

Ghyas Ahmed Gaddi

Ghyas Ahmed Gaddi (1928-1986) is regarded as one of the pillars of Urdu fiction. His prominent short stories, many of which have been translated into many languages are 'Babalog', 'Sea and the Sky' (*Aasman aur Samander*), 'The Murder of Buds' (*Kalyon ka Khoon*), 'The Wheel' (*Pahiya*), 'The Thirsty Bird' (*Pyasi Chirhya*), 'Neighbours and Shadows' (*Saaye aur Hamsaye*), 'The Jasmine Plant' (*Joohi ka Pauda*), 'The Day's End' (*Subah ka Daaman*) etc. His stories portray all the bitterness, failures, and afflictions that define modern man's existence. Ghyas weaves a complex pattern of symbolism and metaphors to present his creative art. He discovers meaning into the small details of life which he shrouds with his symbols and images.

Basically, Ghyas is an allegorical writer. His stories present age old concepts of decency, decorum and moral fibre as central values of life. He is the defender of those values and very rarely does he divert from them in his creative writings. Sometimes his idealism burdens his story line as in the story 'The Landscape and Behind' (*Manzar Pasmanzar*). He sometimes takes help of the *fallback* technique, sometimes symbolism, and in some stories he uses allusions and references. Through all these devices Ghyas projects his modern art through which he delineates his characters and their life.

Devendra Issar

Devendra Issar (b.1928) writes both in Hindi and Urdu. He doesn't write much in Urdu now; nevertheless he is a very powerful writer. His stories also conjure up memories and unravel, the mysteries of existence, the flux of time and tide in a man's life, and the utter sense of what is lost in that process. What is abiding in *Issar's* art is his hold on life and its sustaining power. Issar is an optimist and a romantic at heart. He declares it, sometimes implicitly, through his art.

In 'The Eve-Afflicted Falcon' (*Sada-e-Shaam ka Zakhmi Parinda*) *Issar* presents the forces of suppression crushing the life of innocence and freedom, till the falcon (the child brutalized) is wounded. But even in the state of affliction his eyes are waiting in hope looking outside or in void waiting for some unseen forces to deliver the world from its present crippling state of existence. *Issar* explores the existence of love and revival, and maintains that amid all the chaos of existence, all the destabilizing forces of modern existence, the spirit of love will ultimately survive.

Kalam Haidari

Kalam Haidari (1930-1994) had been on the forefront of Urdu short-story writing since 1950. His earlier works moved around tales of romance and love, but his later works represent the influences of progressivism which as a literary movement was taking its last breath with the advent of '*modernism*' in Urdu literature. His short stories, 'The Rest of Night' (*Raat*

Kitni Baqi Hai), 'Streets Unnamed' (*Benaam Galiyan*), and 'The Barn and the Bars' (*Khaliyan aur Salakhein*) portray the tragic atmosphere of exploitation and brutality.

He later came under the influence of the modern literary movement and 'Zero' (*Sifar*), the new collection of his short stories, portrays the negative energies released by people with power and pelf resulting in negative outcomes for the ruled and the subdued. The emergence of the modern phenomena of doubts, encapsulating time, nihilism, death of values, revolt against wisdom and reason, in short all elements of existentialism are to be discovered in his short stories of this period.

Ilyas Ahmed Gaddi

Ilyas Ahmed Gaddi (1932-1997), novelist and short story writer, born in Bihar, made his literary debut in 1948 with his short story 'Broodings' (*Afkaar*). He published two collections of short stories, two novellas, 'Love has no Compulsions' (*Ishq per zor nahin*), and 'Captivity' (*Aseeri*), and a novel 'Fire Area' which portray life and its moral conflicts in the coalfields of Bihar. With its rootedness in the soil of Bihar, its effective exploitation of the local idiom, and its powerful plea for social justice and humanism, his novel was hailed as a significant addition to Urdu fiction. The novel was awarded with the Sahitya Akademi Award in 1997, a few months before his death.

Like his elder brother Ghyas, Ilyas is also a very cautious writer, and therefore desists from taking any liberty with either the form or content of Urdu fiction. But he succeeds in building up a tragic atmosphere around his story. He is a mood setter, and creates the backdrop as a kind of sub-plot which reinforces the main plot and storyline of his stories.

Khalida Husain

Khalida Husain's (b.1938) short stories are avant-garde in their treatment of the subject. Most of her stories are abstractly psychological, but unfolding the dilemma of existence and, the feeling of isolation in a very telling way. *Khalida Husain* draws her experiences from existential realities, and internalizes them in her stories, through her portrayal of realistically incomprehensible events, and a very subjective diction. 'Adam's Brood' (*Ibn-e-Adam*) is a story where *Hussain* has hitched her wagon to the portrayal of a kind of world where barbarity, intoxication of power, the loss of judgement to separate the right from the wrong, all have combined to push humanity to the bottom edge of existence.

In her stories, *Khalida Husain* delves into the vicissitudes of life and discovers how the tortuous, pervasive maze of memory leads to a growing sense of loss, so much so that the entire existence becomes a kind of prison, an escape from where is a remote possibility. *Khalida Husain* is a fascinating story teller. She mingles with a great ingenuity of thought and expression, the weird and hallucinatory experiences that her characters go through, and their frustrations at discovering that life is a black hole, strange, dark, inexplicable, sucking all that is living, down into it.

Shaukat Hayat

Shaukat Hayat (b. 1950) is a contemporary short story writer and a modernist in the real sense. His works display a painful picture of the hollowness of life, of the severe break down of all oral and human values, of bitter self-realization and the resulting despondency, and inferiority complex, and of the loss of hope in living values. His characters pass through the changing vicissitudes of life, and are lost in the whirlpool of untoward experiences.

Shaukat Hayat's stories 'The Wreck and the Heartbreak' (*Tootney Bikherney ka Almiya*), 'The Wilted Existence' (*Bakson sey Daba Admi*), '*Pendulum*', 'The Black Pigeon on the Green Ridge' (*Sabz Munder per Sayah Kabooter*), '*Hostel*', 'Between the Poles Caught in the Winds' (*Qutbain key Beech Hawaon ki zad Mein*), 'The Paper Tree' (Kaghaz ka Darakht), and 'The Human Carcass' (*Insaani Dhancha*) are, among others, remarkable insights into the man's art and genius. They betray his acute feelings and disturbing realization of man's weaknesses and impotence in the face depressing existential realities.

Asif Farrukhi

Asif Farrukhi (b.1959) is a doctor by profession, and a writer and translator by instinct. An award winning short story writer, his stories portray the bleakest corners of relationships. He explores those bonds that do not always tie. They are often despairing and disgusting. *Asif* is an astute story teller, and is a writer with a tremendously creative imagination. His stories are symbolic, and his symbolism is essentially iconoclastic. In *Bonsai*, the plant that is prevented from reaching its normal size is symbolic of the dwarfed existence of man. The character in the story lives virtually among his plants, and realizes that growth and blossoming is essential for existence, but he discovers that the existential reality thwarts any attempt to grow and sprout. He establishes man's symbiotic relationship with the bonsai plant only to discover that his destiny is tied with it, as both of them are waiting for someone to untie the knot that prevents blossoming.

Asif is a very introspective poet too, and his voice is the voice of the postmodern world—a world where man faces two diametrically opposed realities, and he is destined to live between them, now being pulled this way, now that.

Abdus Samad

Abdus Samad's (b. 1952) short stories present a saga of relationships and identities. He writes about social conflicts, human relationships, and political forces, all presented to be pitted against the exploitation of the common man, the helpless sufferer. A recipient of the Urdu *Sahitya Akademi Award*, from the Indian Academy of Letters, *Abdus Samad* is immensely capable of reconstructing political, social, and even personal experiences to express the plight of man, his loneliness, and the sense of a hopeless loss of identity.

'The Strong Tether-Pin' (*Mazboot Khoonta*) doesn't have any political undertone. The story is essentially about human relationships. In this story *Abdus Samad* creates a world where materialistic concerns and the rush of modern life have made it impossible to understand the voice of true love and humane feelings. Abdus Samad weaves a tapestry of images and stories drawn shuttling between the past and the present around the two characters, and creates a symphony of meanings between them. The central character in the story suffers to witness these two extreme poles of existential reality, and realizes that what appears to be meaningful becomes meaningless, and that which had stood inconsequential, begins imposing itself. Abdus Samad's art probes this strange vagary of life.